He Makes Me Smile

Dedication

For Kevin
who always makes me smile

The steps of the godly are directed by the LORD.
He delights in every detail of their lives.

Psalm 37:23 (NLT)

Chapter One

Dear Lora,

How are you? Thanks for the card you sent me. It came at the perfect time. How's Eric? I hope you're not getting too stressed with wedding plans. I'm so excited for you, and hearing you sound so happy makes me believe in God's constant guidance and presence even more.

My life has been a little crazy lately, but everything seems to be working out for the best. Softball has started, and I'm having a lot of fun this year. I can't believe graduation is only two months away.

I wanted to share one thing with you God has been teaching me. Do you remember that study Daisy told us about where you look at the specific words of Jesus and try to hear what they mean for us right now? Well, I've been doing that since last summer, and recently I read John 14:14 that says, "You may ask me for anything in my name, and I will do it." I never really understood that before and said 'In Jesus' Name' at the end of my prayers because that's what I had been taught to do. But I think what Jesus is saying is He wants us to pray with confidence, to pray in the name of the one who can do the impossible, in the name of the one who can do anything when we trust Him completely. Maybe not exactly like we think He should, but in the very best way.

So I've been praying for myself a lot, that He would make me who He wants me to be, and for whoever He lays on my heart, and then believing He's in control and whatever He does, and however He does it, it's going to be amazing! You seem to be on my heart a lot lately, and you can believe I'm praying for whatever you're going through right now.

Just wanted to share that. Have a great day!

Amber

Sending off the email to Lora, Amber hoped all was well with her. She had received a card with a short note from her the same day she had returned from California and learned Seth had come home early from Mexico. Lora's little note about clinging to joy and peace by putting hope in Jesus had brought her the peace she needed, and since Lora hadn't been writing her much, she knew God had brought her the encouraging words when she most needed them.

The phone rang, and she picked it up. She was the only one in the house at the moment. Her mom and dad had gone out to feed the horses.

"Hello?"

"Hi, babe."

"Hi," she said, feeling surprised to hear from Seth so soon. She had just seen him last night after their romantic anniversary day together.

"I can't stop thinking about yesterday," he said.

She smiled. "Me neither."

In addition to taking a romantic canoe ride, everything they had done had seemed more special after what they had gone through during the last three weeks. Seth loved her in spite of the traumatic 48 hours she had put him through, and after thinking he had lost her, Seth seemed to want to be close to her and hold her more than usual.

"I have some good news and some bad news," he said. "Which would you like first?"

"Bad," she said, wondering if this had anything to do with Matt and Mandy.

"I talked to Matt this morning, and he doesn't want to take Mandy to Prom."

"Why not?" she whined.

"That's the bad news. The good news is he hasn't stopped thinking about her, and he would like to pursue something, but he wants to get to know her better before actually asking her out."

"How is he going to get to know her if he never sees her?"

"Hold on," he laughed. "He knows she's quiet and sensitive, and he wants to make sure his feelings for her go beyond a little infatuation on a weekend retreat. He doesn't want to ask her to go to the prom with him—which we all know would be a huge deal for Mandy—and then discover he's not interested in anything beyond friendship. Don't you agree she would be devastated if he never asked her out again after that?"

"Yes, I suppose. What's he planning to do? Wait until we're all at Lifegate next fall?"

"Yes and no. He probably won't ask her out until then, but he would like to see her a few times before that."

"When?"

"We have some youth activities coming up you could come to with me and invite Mandy to come too, and then maybe this summer she could come along with us on Saturdays sometimes. That way it would be like she's coming along with you but Matt happens to be there too. Matt doesn't want it to be like we're setting them up, but have a chance to get to know her better without her knowing he likes her."

"I suppose that's good thinking," she said, knowing Matt was right about asking Mandy to Prom being too big of a step at this point. "It sounds like he must have more than infatuation going on if he's passing up an opportunity to see her in a great dress and dance with her all evening."

"I think he does. He hasn't talked about her since the retreat, but when I mentioned her today, it was obvious he's been thinking about her."

"Did you tell him she likes him?"

"No. I asked if he was thinking of asking anyone to Prom, and he said 'no', so I said, 'What about Mandy?', and he said he'd thought about it but didn't want to for the reason I told you."

"And he's not planning to ask anyone else?"

"No. I don't think so. He didn't mention anyone else."

"What activities are coming up with your youth group?"

"Next Saturday—paint ball. Matt's definitely going, but I'm guessing that's not Mandy's thing?"

"I doubt it," she said.

"We're going to a concert on the 21st."

"That might be a possibility," she said, checking her calendar. "I have a softball tournament that day, but it should be over by four."

"And on May 5th, we're going to the beach, but I know that's the same day as Prom for your school. Have we decided what we're doing on that?"

Amber thought for a moment and replied honestly. "I don't think I want to go this year. Is that okay?"

"You mean not at all—yours or mine?"

"I had a really nice time last year, but none of my friends are going—unless Mandy gets asked sometime in the next few weeks, and if she's not going, I'd rather not, unless you really want to."

"I'd much rather give Matt and Mandy the chance to see each other again, and we could still go to mine the following weekend, but it's fine if you don't want to. I'd be happy with a quiet walk around the lake instead."

"Me too."

"Are you sure? Or are you saying that because I haven't asked you right?"

"No. I'm sure. It's a lot of money and preparation for one night, and I don't feel right about it after what Mandy said to me. Not getting asked to Prom is twice as worse when your closest friends are going—I know that from experience."

"Have you told her Matt likes her?"

"No, and it's killing me not to, but I know I should let Matt speak for himself."

"Let's plan on going to the beach then. You could invite Chris and Colleen and anyone else too if you want to make it less obvious."

"Okay. I'll ask her about the concert too."

"I'll come out for your games and then drive us in so you won't have to ride MAX, and then you and Mandy could spend the night here."

"And she could see Matt on Sunday too."

"That's true," he laughed. "I wouldn't have pegged you as the matchmaking type when I first met you."

"That's because I wasn't."

"Why the change?"

"I don't know. I guess because I'm in love and it's so great, I want everyone else to be too."

"There's nothing wrong with that, but we need to let God do things in His time, not ours. Don't get frustrated if Matt doesn't make his move until sometime next year, all right?"

"All right. I'll try to be patient. And I do appreciate him wanting to make sure it's right before he charges ahead. I'd rather have him never ask her out than ask her too soon and dump her a week later."

"I think he knows that."

"What's that mean?"

He laughed. "The first thing Matt said after telling me he liked her was, 'But I'm sure Amber won't approve of me getting anywhere near her.'"

Amber felt shocked. "Why would he say that?"

"Because of the way he acted in front of you with Clarissa at the Winter Dance. He's not too sure you approve of *me* being his friend, let alone your very sweet cousin."

"And you let him think that?"

"No. I've told him you're praying for a good girl for him and that you don't hold grudges or judge people for their mistakes, but it's hard for him to believe considering the way he acted that night."

"And you can't tell him otherwise because then he will know you've talked to me about Mandy."

"Yes."

"Keep reminding him of what I really think, okay? I'd hate to see him delay something with Mandy because he thinks I'm thinking things I'm not. If you end up telling him at some point I know about this, tell him I think he would be perfect for Mandy—so much so that I'm writing a story about it!"

"You need to let me read some of what you're writing," he said.

"I will."

"When?" he challenged her. So far she had been putting him off. She thought what she'd written so far was good, but she was also learning a lot as she went and didn't feel ready for others to read it yet.

"Soon," she said.

"How soon?"

She laughed.

"Please? Just a little bit. One chapter."

"No fair asking me over the phone. You'll get me to say yes and then I'll want to take it back later."

"I'll make you a deal."

"What?"

"If you and Mandy end up coming in for the concert and things go halfway decently between her and Matt, then you leave your laptop with me, and I'll read some before I go to sleep. It will be like our private signal of how much you think Mandy enjoyed her time with him."

She supposed she could deal with that. "Okay, but you have to be honest with me. If you think it's awful, I want you to tell me. Can you do that?"

"No."

She laughed. "I'm serious. I don't want to be wasting my time with this if I'm just bad at it."

"I highly doubt that, Amber, but even if you are, you should keep doing it anyway as long as you're enjoying yourself. I have a bunch of stuff I've written that no one will ever see, but it was valuable to me at the time. You don't need to have readers to be a writer."

She knew he was right. She had begun to allow herself to have some lofty dreams, but if none of them came true, she was having fun. Writing relaxed her and brought a unique joy to her heart.

"You can sweet-talk your way into anything."

"It's not sweet-talk. It's true."

"I know. That's even worse!"

He laughed and they talked for another fifteen minutes before he said he needed to go. She thought about calling Mandy and asking her about the concert, but she thought Mandy might be suspicious about why she was asking her now instead of waiting until she saw her at school tomorrow.

She ended up not mentioning it until the following Sunday, which about killed her, but she was able to say it casually, like Seth had mentioned it to her when they spent their usual time together on Saturday.

"Bethany Dillon? Are you serious?"

"Yes. Do you like her?"

"Yes! Can I come with you? Really?"

"Sure you can. That's why I mentioned it."

Mandy was excited and didn't seem to be thinking about Matt, so Amber didn't say anything about him being there too.

"Seth said we could spend the night at his house and then he will bring us back after church on Sunday. Will you be all right with that?"

"Sure," she said. She paused a moment and then spoke again. "You know, I've been thinking a lot about what you said—about being comfortable with my quiet personality, and I think you're right. For a long time I've been trying to be someone I'm not, or at least wishing I was different, but I think I need to accept this is who God made me to be and believe He did for a reason."

Amber recalled something Seth had told her yesterday, and she smiled. When Seth told Matt that Mandy might be going to the concert, Seth asked him what he remembered about her from the short time they had spent together on the retreat, and Matt said, "She didn't talk very much, but I remember everything she said. I can still hear her voice and see her blue eyes that spoke to me without her having to say a thing."

Chapter Two

With an unusually warm and dry spring continuing into the first week of league softball games, Amber and her teammates traveled twice that week, to Parkrose on Monday and to Barlow on Wednesday. Much to their delight they won both games. In recent years Sandy hadn't done so well in softball, usually finishing near the bottom of their league, but last year they had won almost half of their games, and they'd only lost one really good player who had been a senior last year.

After playing softball together for the past three years, their big group of seniors, along with several good juniors and sophomores, seemed to have the makings of a good team. Amber had thought so during the past few weeks of practice and non-league games, but seeing them beat some strong teams in their league confirmed it.

Friday was their greatest test. Centennial, the school that had placed top in their league the past three years, came to their home field. Watching them warm-up before the game intimidated Amber. She had been on varsity the last two years, and they had never beat them—most teams in the Mt. Hood League hadn't. She hadn't pitched well against them either. They were too good. Most of the girls could hit anything.

Her one comfort was Seth being here. She used to be nervous about playing in front of him, but now she always felt better if she knew he was watching her. It gave her a calm feeling and reminded her this was supposed to be fun. And he wasn't the only member of her fan club tonight. Her mom and dad were here, along with her grandma, Uncle Tom and Aunt Beth, Mandy, Colleen, and Nicole. Ben and Hope were coming home this weekend because of Easter being this Sunday, and they were going to try and make it too, but she didn't think they were here yet.

She hadn't asked them all to come. With the warm spring weather, everyone seemed to be in the mood to go to her first home game of the season, and she was happy to have them here. After playing softball for the last ten years, she wanted to enjoy this final season as much as possible. Lifegate wasn't much of an athletic school. They had soccer, tennis, and cross-country teams that competed with other small colleges, but everything else was intramural, and she didn't know if she would play anything there. For her, playing sports had always been more about who she was playing with, and she didn't think volleyball or softball would be the same without Stacey.

When her longtime teammate and friend came out to talk to her on the mound for a moment before the game got underway, Stacey reminded her of something. "We always said we were going to get these guys one year. I think it's about time, don't you?"

"All things are possible, right?"

"I'm behind you all the way, Ambs. Not to mention God and Seth and your whole fan club up there."

"Yo, Amber!" she heard at that same moment. Turning toward the sound, she saw Ben and Hope had arrived. She waved at them and then looked back at Stacey.

"All right then, let's go," she said.

"Would you like me to pray for you?"

Amber stared at Stacey for a moment, wondering if she'd heard right. Stacey had never said that to her before.

"Right now?"

"Yes, now," Stacey said as if she couldn't possibly mean any other time.

"I would love for you to pray for me, Stacey. Thank you."

Stacey took her free hand into hers, bowed her head, closed her eyes, and prayed for her right there in the middle of the infield for all to see. And it was definitely the kind of prayer only Stacey would say.

"Well, Jesus, here we are. The first home game of our senior year, and me and Ambs are still together as teammates and friends like you planned it from the beginning. I know this is just a game with no real significance in the overall scheme of life, but for me and Amber right now, this is a special moment, and I know you understand that. Help us to play our best today. Keep Amber from hurting herself. And if there's any way we can see you more clearly through this little game we're playing, our eyes are open and waiting for you to come shining through. Thanks for all the fun times, Jesus. We'll take some more today if that's your plan. Amen."

"Amen," Amber echoed, smiling at Stacey before she turned away and jogged toward home plate.

Normally she was very serious when it came to pitching, but she couldn't stop smiling for the entire first inning. Every girl who came up to bat had that look of fierce determination in her eyes, ready to smack the ball like there was no tomorrow. But she just smiled at them and then lowered her eyes to Stacey, imagined her friend smiling back at her behind her catcher's mask, and before she knew it, she had struck out two batters and the final one made contact with the ball but couldn't make it to first base before Paige scooped the ball up in the infield and tossed it to Robyn for the third out.

"All right, Amber," she heard Paige say, coming up behind her as they headed for the dugout. "Looks like you have some angels helping you out today. Tell them not to stop."

Amber didn't respond with anything besides another smile, and when Stacey smacked a home run off of her first pitch a few minutes later and scored two runs for them with only one out in the first inning, Amber cheered along with the rest of her teammates and had tears streaming down her cheeks as if they had just won the State Championship. Stacey's dream had always been to hit a home run against this team, and she had never done it until now.

The rest of the game was fun too. They ended up losing by two runs, but that was quite an accomplishment against this team. Amber would have loved to win, but she played well and so did Stacey, and afterwards they hugged each other, and Stacey said, "I'm going to miss this next year, Amber. I'm going to miss you."

"We've got a few more months to go," she said. "We'll make the most of them, okay?"

"Okay, Princess Amber. You've got it."

Their whole team, along with family and friends, went to Paola's for pizza after the game, and something very interesting happened. She and Seth were sitting at a table with Stacey, Mandy, Paige, and two other girls on their team, along with one of the girl's boyfriends. Amber didn't know if Paige was dating anyone right now, but if she was, he wasn't here.

Paige had never met Seth before, and she introduced herself when she sat across from him at the end of the table. He had been at some of her softball games last year, and Amber knew Paige had seen him, but she had never had the opportunity to meet him before.

"I've heard a lot of good things about you, Seth," Paige said, speaking to him in a sweet and polite manner, much like she would talk to a teacher or her friends' parents. "Where do you live exactly? I know Amber told me, but I can't remember."

"Portland," he said. "Near the zoo."

"What do you think of our little town out here in the mountains?"

"There's one thing about it I like very much," he said, turning to look at her.

Amber returned his warm smile, and Seth surprised her by giving her a sweet kiss. He did that all the time in front of her family and close friends, but in groups he tended to hold back more. Amber glanced at Paige, and she saw a look on her face she had never seen before: A look of envy. But rather than feeling triumphant that she had a great boyfriend and Paige didn't—like she often wanted to feel around popular girls like Paige, she had a feeling of extreme sadness sweep through her, and she saw Paige's brokenness.

She had it all together on the outside—beautiful, athletic, tons of friends, college-bound, a laugh a minute—but on the inside she was missing the thing she needed most: To know she was loved. Not by a boyfriend necessarily, but by anyone, especially God.

Amber had been praying for her teammates, but she had no idea how to reach them with the message of God's love. In many ways she felt like a missionary in a foreign country right in her own high school. Paige and her friends spoke a different language than she did. They were part of a different culture she couldn't relate to: divorced homes, growing up without any clear moral teaching, parents who were more messed up than they were, bits and pieces of different philosophies and religions they had heard. To her the truth of God was second nature, something that had become a part of who she was without her fully understanding all of it.

But for someone like Paige, Jesus was as foreign to her as Queen Elizabeth. It would be like trying to convince Paige she needed to become British. Amber's heart went out to her, but she had no idea what to do about it. She said a silent prayer, like she had done many times, but she didn't have any reason to think anything significant would happen now.

Paige asked Seth a few more questions.   Amber knew they were oblivious to her silent plea for God to reach Paige in the middle of the noisy room. Part of her was saying, 'This isn't the time or place.' And another part of her could imagine Jesus seeing it as the perfect time and place.

"What are you planning to major in?" Paige asked Seth. She had already asked him about his college plans and learned they were going to Lifegate together.

"Youth Ministry," Seth replied.

"What's that?"

"Helping teenagers find God."

"Wow," Paige said with a laugh. "I haven't heard that one before."

Seth didn't respond to her comment directly but asked where she was going to college and what she was planning to major in.

"I haven't decided for sure, but I think I'm going to OSU, and I want to study psychology."

"My brother goes there."

"Oh? What year is he?"

"A sophomore. Why do you want to study psychology?"

"So I can help people with their problems. I do that already, I just want to get paid for it!"

"You and I aren't that different then," Seth said. "Except for the method, we both want to help others."

"What do you mean—the method?" Paige asked.

Seth answered matter-of-factly. "You'll learn all about ways people think and behave and use that to help them with their problems, and I'll pretty much do the same thing with God factored into it—helping them find God and looking to Him for help rather than using their own resources."

"What difference can God make?"

"Tons," Seth said with a laugh. "I'd be completely lost without Him, aren't you?"

Paige was speechless. Amber was in awe of Seth's ability to bring the conversation to this point. Seth appeared fearless and confident. And they both waited for Seth to say something else.

"Sorry," Seth said. "I didn't mean to assume you don't know God. Do you?"

"I don't even know what you mean by that," Paige said.

"Do you believe in God?"

"Yeah, I guess."

"Do you want to know Him?"

"I don't know. Maybe. What do you mean by knowing Him?"

"Knowing what He's like, having a relationship with Him, letting His love be a part of your heart."

Their conversation was interrupted by the pizzas being delivered to the table. Seth didn't press further. They all reached for a slice and began eating. Seth seemed to be letting the subject hang out there, waiting for Paige to comment further.

Amber glanced at Seth, and he winked at her. Mandy was sitting on her other side, and Amber didn't know if she had been able to hear Seth and Paige's conversation. It was really noisy. The place was always packed on a Friday night. But when Mandy leaned over and whispered something in her ear, she knew Seth's voice had carried at least that far.

"If it was me, I'd want to know."

Amber silently agreed. Seth had a way of talking about God that made Him so real and appealing. Kara, one of Paige's friends who was sitting a few seats away, came down to tell her something, and Paige turned her attention elsewhere, but Amber could tell she still had one eye on Seth. She seemed to be waiting for him to say something else, but he remained silent.

It wasn't until they were all leaving that Paige said something to Seth directly. They had all been talking and laughing, jumping from one subject to the next, but before they left the table, Paige handed something to Seth—a napkin with writing on it.

"I'd like to talk with you more about what you were saying earlier," she said. "That's my email address. If you feel like writing me sometime, I'd like that, okay?"

"Sure, Paige. I'll do that."

"Bye, Amber. See you Monday."

"Bye, Paige. Have a nice weekend."

Paige stepped away without saying anything else. Amber watched her go and then looked at Seth. "I think I'm in love with you."

"That wasn't me, Amber. That's God."

"Well, I'm in love with Him too."

He pulled her close to him and held her gently. *"The one who existed from the beginning is the one we have heard and seen. We saw him with our own eyes and touched him with our own hands. He is Jesus Christ, the Word of life."*

Chapter Three

The following afternoon Amber and Seth wrote an email to Paige together. Seth mostly wrote it, and Amber suggested a couple of changes based on some things she knew about Paige. Amber read it over one final time before Seth sent it off.

Dear Paige,

It was nice meeting you last night and getting to know you a little bit. I'm glad you're interested in continuing our discussion about the difference God can make in your life. And I want you to know I'm not trying to push my beliefs on you. For me, God is my life, and He makes such a huge difference for me, I want others to experience that, but I will leave your pursuit of Him entirely up to you.

Since you don't seem to know much about God, I'll start at the beginning and try to make it as simple as possible, which is easy in some ways because God has made it easy for us to know Him, but He's also complex and mysterious at times, and by no means do I have Him completely figured out. But basically, God is our creator. He made us, and He made the world. How do I know that? Well, there's no way to know for sure—it's not like any of us

were there—but the Bible tells us that's the way it happened, and I believe it because there are a lot of other things in the Bible I have seen ring true in my life, and I also believe it because I think this world is too beautiful and amazing for it to have happened all on its own. If you want to know God, you have to believe Him, and that begins with believing He exists and that He made you. Once you are willing to explore that possibility, you can take the next step to knowing Him.

If He does exist, why can't we see Him or hear Him, you may ask? When God created the world and the first people, everything was perfect. A real-life Paradise where nature was in harmony with itself in every way and people were perfect. No hate. No deceit. Completely loving with each other and with God. There were no barriers between God and people. He walked and talked with them in the beautiful world He had created for them.

But then something happened. God had made a garden for the first people to live in, and He told them they could eat any of the fruit in the garden for food, except for one tree. That tree was off-limits. God said, 'Don't eat from that tree or you will die.' You may have heard the story: Eve ends up taking a bite of the apple, or whatever it was, and then Adam does too. The Bible says they sinned against God, which basically means they didn't do what God said. They didn't obey, and so they were separated from God and died just like God said. They lived for awhile, had a bunch of children and grandchildren, or you and I wouldn't be here today, but eventually they got old and died, which isn't the way God intended when He created them initially. He created them to live forever in a perfect world and in perfect relationship with Him, but because they didn't believe God and do what He said, it could no longer be that way.

So what does all that have to do with you and me? Pretty much everything. We are not perfect people. We are separated from God like they were, and eventually we all die. And not only do we die physically someday, but we're already dead spiritually right now. Without having a connection to God, we are dead on the inside. That's just the way God made us—to know Him; and if we don't, then we're empty and lost. We don't know God or understand Him. We don't know and understand ourselves most of the time. We make bad choices and we end up lonely, confused, hurt by others, hurting others ourselves, hating people, breaking up with someone we once loved, getting caught up in the pursuit of money and success and popularity and whatever else, but never feeling happy and satisfied.

Do you ever feel that way? I bet you do if you don't know God. And I feel that way sometimes too. I'm not perfect. I make mistakes. I sometimes get lost. But only when I stop listening to God and doing what He says.

These are some ways I have seen God make a difference in my life, just to name a few: I have a good relationship with my parents; I have an awesome relationship with Amber; I have direction for the future and in my everyday life; I believe God loves me and has a special purpose for me; Basically I'm a happy person who loves life, and even when things aren't going my way, I know God is in control and everything is going to be okay because He loves me and will never abandon me. And I have no fear of death because when I die, I know I will be with Him.

Yesterday I asked if you believe in God, and I hope you will think about that and make a decision about whether you want to or not. If you don't, that's your choice and I respect that. But if you do—or at least think you might want to, then you can write and tell me so, and I'll explain more about how you can know Him. Again, it's a simple thing, and yet it takes some time to explain. I don't want to overload you too much with a bunch of new information to think about.

But I do believe in Him, and I know Him pretty well, and I can tell you with absolute certainty that He loves you, Paige, very much. And He wants you to know Him and discover the huge difference He can make in your life.

Sincerely,
Seth

He created everything there is. Nothing exists that He didn't make. Life itself was in Him, and this life gives light to everyone. (John 1:3-4—The Bible)

After sending the email, Seth wanted them to pray for Paige together, and so they did. They both were hopeful Paige would write back and ask about how she could know God, but if she didn't, Amber knew God was doing what she had asked for. She had asked God to reveal Himself to Paige, and He was doing that in a way she had never imagined.

"This is what our life is going to be about, isn't it?" she said. "Living our lives together, trusting God, and helping others to find Him?"

"I hope so," Seth said.

"You know what surprises me most about growing up?"

"What?"

"I always had this vision of becoming independent and free to live my life however I wanted, but the older I get, the more I realize how much I need everyone around me and how much I need to depend on God."

"I know exactly what you mean," he said, giving her a sweet kiss. "But I think it should be fun, don't you?"

"If we keep seeking God and going where He leads us."

"Yes, we'll do that. It's been working out great so far."

She smiled at him. "Two seeking hearts are stronger than one."

"Do you still have that poem?"

"Of course I do. I'm hanging on to that one forever."

"Can I see it?"

"Don't you have a copy?"

"No. I gave you the only one."

They were in her room, sitting on the floor where they had been writing to Paige on her laptop. She went to her desk and pulled the stack of poems from their place and returned to sit beside him. They were in an old stationary box with a red satin ribbon tied around them, and she undid the bow and then glanced at Seth. She could feel his eyes on her. He had the strangest look on his face.

"What?"

"Are those all the poems I've written for you?"

"Yes. I told you I've kept every one. You didn't believe me?"

"No, I believed you. I just imagined them stuffed into a drawer, not in a special box with a ribbon tied around them."

"Stuffed into a drawer?" She smiled and shook her head. "No way, Seth Kirkwood. These poems are my treasures."

He stared at her, appearing as though he might cry, and she couldn't believe he didn't realize how much they meant to her. She loved all of his letters, but these poems came from another place in his heart—a place he only opened for her.

She took the Seeking Hearts poem from its place. Handing it to him, she asked him to read it to her out loud. He read it slowly and with a hint of nostalgia for their early days together.

"Two seeking hearts are stronger than one
And it's hard to believe He's only begun
To weave our hearts together into one, don't you see?
I believe that's what He's doing between you and me

I never imagined it would be like this
So pure and right, nothing but bliss
You're invading my heart so easy and fast
And I hope and pray the blue skies will last

We'll seek Him together, not just apart
We'll share our thoughts, we'll share our hearts
We'll learn His truth and live it out
I want us to shine and maybe even shout

That His love is real and it is here
Within our hearts it becomes clear
This isn't a mistake or just random chance
He wants us to live, He wants us to dance

And so we will dance, my jewel, my treasure
Not with meaningless talk and mere fleeting pleasure
But by seeking things above: His love and His heart
Yes, Amber, I believe this is only the start"

"Do you remember writing that?"

He smiled. "Yes, I remember."

"What's that smile for?"

"At the time I remember thinking, 'You can't give that to her. It's way too deep.' But I also knew I didn't want anything less in a relationship, and I knew God gave it to me to show me what He wanted for us. I just wasn't sure if it was realistic."

"I believed it was," she said, taking the paper from his fingertips. "You made me believe it, and then you lived up to it—you still are in every way."

They heard footsteps on the stairs, and they both looked toward the hallway to see Ben step onto the landing and then into the open doorway. Ben and Hope had been downstairs studying together for the last hour while she and Seth had been up here.

"You two about ready?" Ben asked. "It's almost three."

The four of them were planning to go to the lake and then into town for a nice dinner. "I'm ready," she said, refolding the poem and putting it in its place on the pile.

"Give us a few minutes," Seth said.

"Okay," Ben replied. "We're ready whenever you are."

Ben stepped away, and Amber looked at Seth, curious as to why he'd said that. They had finished writing the email to Paige, which was the main reason they were up here, and he had finished reading the poem, so it wasn't like Ben had interrupted anything, but Seth had something else to say.

He kissed her first, and it was a little bit different than usual. She always enjoyed his sweet affection, but this seemed to come from a deeper place in his heart. A place of longing and desire, and yet was in no way lustful or more than she was comfortable with. It took her breath away and made her see how much Seth loved being with her. He had always been good about telling her and showing her exactly how he felt, and that's what he seemed to be doing, wanting to express it because he couldn't hold it inside.

"I love you so much, Amber." His voice sounded lonely, like she was the only person in his life. "You know that, right? You know how much I need you? How much I cherish you? How much I love being in love with you? How much I treasure every moment we have together?"

She let the tears fall. Just when she thought Seth couldn't make her feel any more loved, his simple words took her to new depths she didn't know existed. It seemed unreal, but the reality of it couldn't be denied. They were living it.

They went downstairs to go with Ben and Hope to the lake. Riding in the back seat of Ben's car, Amber snuggled into Seth's side and remained there until they arrived. She reattached herself to him when they reached the lake's edge

34

and began walking along the path. He didn't seem to mind her clinginess. She wasn't usually like this, but she couldn't help it.

About halfway around the lake, Seth stopped walking and kissed her. Ben and Hope were ahead of them, and Seth took full advantage of the private but safe setting, kissing her the same way he had been earlier.

"You've got me all messed up, Amber," he said, revealing his thoughts once again. "I had my plan all worked out, and then you turned it upside-down in three short weeks."

"What plan?"

"The plan to keep our relationship growing at a steady pace, enjoying a fun and meaningful summer with you at camp, and then heading off to college as this steady couple with stars in our eyes but our feet on the ground, making wise and mature decisions on our own for the first time."

"How have I messed that up?"

"You made me think I'd lost you. For two days I thought about our relationship, trying to figure out where I went wrong, and the more I thought about it, the more I realized how much a part of my heart you had become."

"How does that affect your plan?"

"You made me fall in love with you all over again. I can't concentrate at school. I can't go five minutes without thinking about you. You're the first thing on my mind when I wake up and the last thought before I go to sleep. And the way I kissed you earlier and right now is the way I've been wanting to kiss you for the last three weeks—ever since you came into my room and sat down beside me. I've kept those feelings and desires to myself, but I can't do it anymore, Amber. I have to show you what's inside my heart."

She smiled. "I don't mind."

He kissed her again, and she allowed herself to enjoy it. Seth's kisses had always been wonderful, but these were beyond anything she had ever experienced before.

"I don't want to go home tonight," he said, pulling her close to him and holding her tight. "I don't want to be away from you ever again."

Welcome to my world, Seth. I've been feeling that way for a year and a half.

"How many more days until we go to camp?"

"Too many," he said.

She laughed and stepped back. She had never seen him like this—so desperate and needy, and she wasn't sure how to handle it. Taking his hand and pulling him along, she said, "Come on, sweet thing. Before the Brother Patrol comes looking for us."

Chapter Four

Seth followed her down the trail, and for the next hour he was the clingy one, holding her close as they walked the remainder of the way around the lake and rode in the car together to their dinner destination. Her mom and dad had encouraged the four of them to go out for a nice dinner somewhere, and they were paying for it as an Easter gift.

As the evening progressed, Amber had the feeling Ben and Hope had something on their minds concerning each other. They didn't appear to be mad or upset about anything, but they weren't quite themselves, especially Hope. Before they all left the restaurant, Amber went to the restroom and Hope did also. She decided to ask her if something was wrong.

"No, we're fine," she said.

"But there is something going on, right?"

"What makes you say that?"

"There's not?"

Hope sighed. "There is, but I can't tell you."

"Okay. But I'm here if you need to talk, all right?"

"I know, Amber. Thanks."

Amber gave her a hug. "Whatever it is, you're safe in God's hands."

Hope didn't respond.

"And I don't mean that as a cliché. You really are, no matter what. Say that to yourself over and over until you believe it with all of your heart."

Hope smiled. "He's certainly shown me that before."

"Can I ask you one thing?"

"Sure."

"Is my brother being a jerk?"

Hope smiled. "No, Amber. He's not. We're not having a problem, we're discussing something."

"Okay. That's all I need to know."

"Pray for us, okay? Me especially."

"I will," she said.

They left the ladies' room and met Ben and Seth outside. They appeared to be having a serious conversation also but let it drop and turned their attention to her and Hope as they approached them. Amber really wanted to know what was going on, and she had a feeling Ben had been telling Seth about it, but she decided to wait and see if Seth said anything.

On the drive home, Seth asked her something, speaking quietly for her ears only. "Do you still love me?"

She smiled at him. "Yes."

"Do you still like me?"

"Yes."

"I think I could use a good love letter from you this week."

She laughed. They had this conversation often, but this time he was speaking the words she usually did. "The last one you got from me wasn't too good, huh?"

"No. Not your best."

"Okay, I'll try to redeem myself, and this time you can believe every single word is true."

He kissed her sweetly. "Speaking of letters, you're going to get one from me on Monday, and I want to warn you that I ask you something serious, and I asked in a letter because I want you to think and pray about it all week, rather than give me the answer you think I want to hear, okay?"

Great. Now I have two things to be wondering about. "Okay," she answered more calmly than she felt. "Should I write you my letter before I get that one, or does it matter?"

He thought for a moment and laughed. "Write me one before you get mine."

She decided she wasn't going to speculate about the letter or about Ben and Hope. She would drive herself crazy with the possibilities, and it would end up being something she'd never thought of anyway. Seth would have to leave shortly after they returned to the house, and she preferred to spend their final minutes together in a different way.

"I love you, Seth. I never stopped. Don't doubt that, okay? That letter was about me and how I was feeling about myself, not how I feel about you. I don't think it's possible for me to fall out of love with you at this point. Even if you stopped loving me, it would take me a long time to get you out of my heart."

"You don't need to worry about that, sweetheart. I'm not stopping."

He kissed her, and she let the tears fall. She never got used to being away from him for a week at a time, and she was really glad they only had a few more weeks of this to go.

She didn't have to wait until Monday to hear from him. He emailed her the following day. Paige had responded to his message, and he shared it with her, along with the reply he had written and wanted her input on.

Dear Seth,

Thank you for your message. I've never heard anybody talk about God like that, and I am interested in knowing more about him and the difference he can make in my life. Like you said, I

feel clueless most of the time about who I am and how I should or want to live my life. I've buried a lot of the pain from my parents' divorce, my bad relationship with my mom, and some hurtful relationships I've been in, but it never goes away entirely, and I'd love to be able to say what you said about being a happy person who loves life, and even when things aren't going my way to know God is in control and everything is going to be okay. I also liked what you said about God loving me. I'm not sure why or how that's possible, but I'd like to hear more about that. There have been days lately, quite a few in fact, when I have felt that no one loves me and I am not lovable. So if you can convince me of that, I'm interested in what you have to say.

Sincerely,
Paige

P.S. Amber has told me a lot about you and the kind of relationship the two of you have, and I figure any guy who is in a relationship for more than just sex is worth listening to. I used to think Amber was naive and just plain stupid at times, but now I see her as one of the smartest and most truly beautiful girls I know. (You can tell her I said that.)

Amber felt tears stinging her eyes, and some of the pain from Paige's hurtful words in the past washed away. She said a silent prayer, thanking God for helping her to speak the truth to Paige and that she was able to say those things about Seth. Then she read Seth's reply.

Dear Paige,

First of all, I have to say I completely agree with you about Amber being very smart and very beautiful. And she would be the first to tell you (after me, of course) that she is the way she is because of believing God loves her and because she seeks after Him with all of her heart. She's not faking anything or just saying nice-sounding words. She lives in the reality of God's love for her every day, and that makes the difference in her life just like it does in mine. I also know she would love to talk to you about God anytime you feel comfortable doing so.

But I also understand your need to perhaps hear about God in this way—through a letter where you can have a chance to read and think about it on your own before talking to someone face to face. As Amber and I have found, letters are a wonderful way to communicate for two main reasons: One because they last forever and you can read them over and over as much as you need to; and two because sometimes the truth is easier to speak and understand through writing than verbal speech. And I think God knows this about letters too, which is why He wrote one for us. In my last message I mentioned the Bible, and basically I think of it as God's love letter to us. The Bible tells us who God is, and who we are, and how we can know Him. And over and over God says, 'I love you. I love you. I love you.'

I grew up hearing stories and words from the Bible, and for years I thought of it as a big rule book that said 'Do this and God will be happy, and don't do this or He won't be.' But now I see it for what it really is—God telling us how to experience life to the full: free from guilt and unnecessary pain, and filled with love and freedom. One example of this is when God tells us to be morally pure. He's not restricting us, but protecting us from the pain and negative consequences of being in a sexually active relationship outside of marriage. I don't know if you know what I'm talking about, but if you do, I think you likely agree there is emotional pain and destruction that goes along with that. And that is definitely not what God wants for us. He wants us to be happy and free from guilt, low self-esteem, and the pain of unhealthy and broken relationships. He created us to love and to be truly loved, and this is completely within our grasp. Not just for me and Amber, but for you too, Paige.

So anyway, the main thing you need to know and understand about God is that we are separated from Him because of our lack of knowledge and belief in Him, but through believing in His forgiveness for our unbelief and mistakes, we can begin a relationship with Him. He can heal our wounds from the past, and we can start fresh and go from there. We can believe He really does love us because He tells us so, and because He showed it. Two thousand years ago, He came to earth as a man named Jesus. He taught people about God's love and power, and He displayed it too. He healed people and raised people from the dead and a bunch of other wild stuff, and then He was killed because of who He claimed to be. But He didn't stay dead. He rose from the dead. (That's the Easter Story.) It might sound crazy, but I believe it's true because it is through my belief in this truth that I am who I am. Jesus (God) now lives within me, not just "out there" somewhere, and He brings me peace, joy, and the ability to know Him. And most of all, He fills my heart with His love—His love for me, and love I can give to others. At the heart of God is His love for us, and the only way to know that is to believe it and experience it for yourself. And the most amazing thing is, it's completely free to whoever wants it. You can't earn it. You can only accept it as a reality.

There's a lot more I could tell you about why it works this way, and I'm willing to do that and answer any questions you have, but I'll leave you with the simplicity of it all for now and encourage you to take some time to think and talk to God on your own. He's right there, Paige, waiting to listen and hear you say, 'I want to know You and receive your love, God. Help me to do that.'

With the love of Jesus,
Seth

P.S. Here's a few words from the Bible I encourage you to read once a day and ask God to speak to you through them. His message for us is both universal (the same for everyone), and personal. He will speak to your heart on a one-on-one basis and show you the difference He can make in YOUR life if you ask Him to.

Don't copy the behaviors and customs of this world, but let God transform you into a new person by changing the way you think. Then you will know what God wants you to do, and you will know how good and pleasing and perfect his will really is. (Romans 12:2)

Chapter Five

Amber responded to Seth by email, saying she thought his response to Paige was perfect, and then she took out some notebook paper and began writing an old-fashioned love letter to him as promised. She took a moment to think about what she wanted to say, but once she got started it all came easily.

Dear Seth,

I know I already told you so in my email, but I think you're amazing for the way you are sharing about Jesus with Paige, and I agree with her that you have a unique way of talking about God and making Him real. You remind me of my dad in that way, and I know God has some very special plans in mind for you, and us, as we seek and serve Him in the coming days, months, and years.

Your relationship with God and the way you live it out in your life has always been the thing that attracted me to you the most. And it is the primary reason I wrote my most recent letter to you. I felt like I didn't deserve to be with someone like you, and I know you would be the first to say you're not perfect or more on-top-of-things spiritually than I am, but from my perspective it often seems that way. But I'm learning to rest in God's grace like never before, and I consider you to be one of the greatest gifts of grace He has ever given me.

Before I wrote that letter I had never once considered breaking up with you. I had never said to myself, 'I'm not sure if I want this guy in my life.' I have often wondered if you really wanted to be with me, or if I deserved you, but I have loved you from the beginning. I still remember the look in your eyes and the sound of your voice that day I spilled my Pepsi on you. Even then you were such a sweet thing, but I never imagined you would be MY sweet thing! Even now I sometimes wonder if it's all been an amazing dream, and I'm going to wake up and realize that my week at camp is just starting. How that week ever turned out the way it did can only be explained by saying what you have told me many times: God planned it. And I am very grateful and amazed that He did.

I love you, Seth. I love everything about you. I love the way you love me. And I love our relationship. I wouldn't change a thing about it, even writing that letter to you. Since then I have fallen more deeply in love with you too, and I thank you from the bottom of my heart for not being mad and accepting my apology without reservation. I promise I will never lie to you again for any reason, even about whatever it is that you have written me this week. And I thank you for always being honest with me, even when difficult issues arise that I know you would rather not say anything about than risk me being mad at you. I will never be mad at you for being honest, even if I don't exactly like what you have to say!

I'm looking forward to our summer together and to going to college with you in the fall. I admit I'm a little worried you are changing your mind about one of those, but I don't think you would tell me something that drastic in a letter. But even if you have, I'm sure you have your reasons, and I will trust God to see me through, and as long as I still have you in my life, I can live with any further separation we must endure. I won't like it, but I won't let you go over it either. I need you in my life, Seth. You are meant to be a part of my heart. I believe that, and I know you do too.

I look forward to the day we will share our lives in every way. But for now I will enjoy this: being in love with you and being your sweetheart and falling in love with you more and more each day.

With a kiss of love,
Amber

On Monday morning Amber mailed the letter to Seth from the mailbox on her way to school with Stacey. She decided not to tell Stacey about the email Seth had sent to Paige or her response, and she also decided not to say anything to Paige about it that afternoon when she saw her at softball practice. If Paige approached her and wanted to talk, she would be happy to do so, but at this point she felt saying anything to her might not be what Paige was ready for. And as long as Paige trusted Seth and was willing to listen to him, she saw no reason to interfere.

She wanted to rush home after softball practice and see if Seth's letter had arrived, but at lunch Mandy asked if she could come over to Grandma's for dinner that evening and then hang around so they could talk. Amber had said she would and had decided she would spend the night there too.

Stacey dropped her off on the way home. She was anxious to hear from Seth, but she was also interested in spending time with Mandy and hearing what she had on her mind. She hadn't seen her since Friday because Mandy had gone to Eugene with her parents for Easter Weekend. Amber had asked her this morning if she'd had a nice time, but Mandy said she would rather wait to share details. After dinner they went to Mandy's room, and she didn't waste any more time to share her news.

"You'll never guess who I saw at church on Sunday."

"Who?" she asked, knowing Mandy was referring to her old church in Eugene.

"Jeremiah Baldwin."

"Who's that?"

Mandy let out a huge sigh and flopped onto her bed. "The guy I want to marry."

Amber laughed. "Since when?"

"Since the first day of camp last summer."

"Did you work with him there?"

"Yes. He's my Seth. I know it."

"What about Matt?" Amber asked before she could stop herself.

Mandy propped herself up on her elbows. "Matt?"

Amber sat down on the bed. "Seth's best friend. You know, the guy you were in love with a month ago."

"I don't even know him. That was just a crush."

"And Jeremiah's different?"

"Yes. I sort of got to know him last summer. Way more than Matt, and he's more quiet, like me."

"Why was he at your old church?"

"He's a friend of T.J.'s. They're at George Fox together, but Jeremiah lives in Portland, so I wouldn't have expected him to come to Eugene with T.J. on Easter Weekend, but his parents are on vacation in Florida right now."

"So he's in college?"

"Yes. He's the same age as T.J."

"Did you talk to him a lot?"

"Yes. He sat beside me in church, and we talked afterwards while Mom and Dad were saying hi to everybody, and then he came to my grandparents' house with T.J. for part of the afternoon until they had to go pick up some friends and drive back to school."

"Is he going to be at camp this summer?"

"Yes! And the coolest thing is I didn't think he was going to be! T.J.'s not, and Jeremiah wasn't going to be either but then a week ago he changed his mind."

"That's great!" Amber said, not knowing what else to say. As far as Mandy knew, there was no reason for her to not be happy with the news, and even if Mandy liked him, that didn't mean they would end up going out, or maybe they would and Jeremiah really was the right guy for her.

"I'm thinking of doing something, and I want your advice," Mandy said.

"What?"

"I'm thinking of writing him a letter and telling him how I feel."

"Now?"

"I want to do it before camp starts, because if he's interested then we can have the whole summer to spend time together, and if he's not, then I won't spend my whole summer wishing and hoping, you know?"

"Yeah, I guess that makes sense," Amber said, hearing the reservation in her voice this time. She had told herself not to, but she had gotten her hopes up for something between Matt and Mandy. Mandy was going to be seeing him in another five days, but if she wrote to Jeremiah this week, that would keep her from allowing anything to happen with Matt this weekend.

"You don't think I should?" Mandy asked.

"I didn't say that. I guess I'm wondering if you want to put your heart out there. What if he says he's not interested and then you have to spend the whole the summer with him. Can you do that?"

Some of Mandy's light faded, and Amber instantly felt bad. *Oh, Jesus, help! What am I supposed to say?*

You can ask Me for anything.

But I don't know what to ask for.

Yes, you do.

Okay, lead Mandy to the right guy for her, and help me to stay out of it!

"Mandy, I'm sorry. That wasn't the right thing to say. I think you should do it if you really want to. Don't let your fears stop you. You're right. It would be better to have the whole summer with him or know it's not meant to be from the beginning. I'm just not used to seeing you be so bold about something!"

Mandy's smile returned somewhat, and Amber decided to leave it at that. If Mandy had the guts to write Jeremiah a letter, then maybe he was the right guy for her.

"I'm scared to death, Amber, but I really feel like I want to do this."

"Then do it. Tonight, before you have a chance to change your mind."

"Actually, I told myself I'd pray about it for a week and decide next Sunday, and I think I should do that. Right now I feel like this is what I want, but I do want to let God lead me to the right guy. I just think He might be asking me to take a step of faith here, you know?"

"Then that's what you should do. Why are you even asking me?"

"Because I value your advice, and if you think I shouldn't, I won't."

Amber restated her words. "I think this is your decision to make, Mandy, and if you want to and don't feel God telling you no, then you should."

Mandy smiled, and Amber saw the hope return to her blue eyes. She asked Mandy to tell her about Jeremiah, and Mandy talked for a long time, giving Amber a reason to believe he may be the right guy for her instead of Matt, and he did sound like a neat guy. He was majoring in youth ministry and wanted to be a youth pastor, just like Seth.

"Do you still want to go to the concert this Saturday?" Amber asked before they got started on their homework.

"Yes! I can't wait."

Amber had to smile. She had never seen Mandy this happy and excited before, and she knew Jeremiah had everything to do with it.

"Do you think Matt will be there?" Mandy asked her.

"At the concert?"

"Yes."

"I think so," she said. "Why?"

Mandy shrugged. "Just wondering."

Amber smiled at her.

"Amber. He's not for me."

"I didn't say anything."

"But you're thinking it."

Amber didn't deny that, but she did voice her other thoughts. "Who you like is up to you, Mandy. Jeremiah sounds like a great guy, and if something happens between the two of you this summer, that's great. But don't count Matt or any guy out just because you think he's out of your league, okay? If I had done that, I would not have Seth."

Mandy didn't respond, and Amber asked her one last thing. "Have you thought about Matt at all since the retreat?"

Mandy smiled. "He's not the kind of guy you forget about."

"But you're certain he hasn't given you another thought."

"I'm nobody, Amber. Just your quiet cousin."

"Not true, Amanda Elizabeth Smith. You want my advice?"

"What?"

"Don't write to Jeremiah until after you see Matt this weekend. And if you can honestly tell yourself you would rather be with him over Matt, then write it, but if you can't, then write a letter to Matt instead."

"Amber!" She laughed. "I can't do that!"

"Why not?"

"Because I can't. And you can't make me!"

"I won't. This isn't about me, Mandy. It's about you. Take my advice, don't take it. I'm just saying there's no reason for Matt to not like you. Did you know he hasn't been on a single date since he broke up with Clarissa? He's not looking for just anybody. He's looking for the right one, and there's absolutely no reason why that can't be you."

Chapter Six

By the time Amber arrived home from softball practice on Tuesday evening, she was going crazy over what she would find in the letter Seth had mentioned over the weekend. Oftentimes she waited until bedtime to read his letters, but she couldn't wait and rushed up the stairs after a quick hello to her mom and dad.

Opening her bedroom door, she saw several pieces of mail lying on her pillow. Two from Seth, one from Lexi, and one from camp. She opened the one from camp first and found what she expected: a letter saying she had been accepted for the summer staff team again this year, something she had been anticipating, but it was nice to know it was official. She had applied to be on counseling staff and hadn't known if they would give that to her, but they had, and she was both scared and excited at the prospect.

Lexi's letter was mostly informative. She had been having a good freshman year at college and things between her and Josh continued to go well. They were both going to be at camp this summer again for sure—they had both received their letters of acceptance on Saturday.

Taking a deep breath, she opened the first letter from Seth, trying to be prepared for anything and reminding herself Seth had never told her any bad or disappointing news in a letter. He always seemed to know how she needed to hear about things, and as she scanned the letter, she knew he had chosen wisely once again. This was the kind of thing he wanted her to think about on her own and then when they saw each other, they would talk about it.

Dear Amber,

I've been thinking about something over the last few weeks, and I've decided it's time for me to tell you about it and see what you think. I really do want this to be a decision we make together, not just something I decide for us, but I feel the need to be honest with you, and please know this has absolutely nothing to do with how I feel about you—that we're getting too serious or anything like that. This is only about what I feel may be necessary to protect our relationship this summer.

With both of us likely being on counseling staff, I know our time together during the week will be very limited. I remember those weeks you were counseling last summer and how much I missed you and looked forward to Saturday coming, and I can imagine that only increasing as the summer goes by. I'm a little bit worried about that. I know me, Amber. And I know how I'm going to want to spend those few precious hours we have together. I'm going to want you all to myself, not to be sharing you with a bunch of other people, but I know that would not be wise, and so I want us to commit together that we will keep our alone-time to a minimum. I'm planning to talk to Ben and to Matt and have them keep me accountable in this because I don't want to leave this all up to me. My desire for you has become much stronger in the last few weeks, and I'm not above asking for help to keep things between us as they should be.

But at the same time I do feel that us having some time alone together is what we will both need. Time where we can talk and share our deepest thoughts like we often did down at the river on Saturday evenings last year, and I'd like to have that time with you again, but with one major change, and this is the part I want you to pray about and share your honest thoughts and feelings with me when we see each other again.

I want us to have a "no kissing" policy for any alone-time we have together this summer. Kissing you in secluded locations has become more and more difficult for me, and unlike being with you here, where I know I need to have you home by a certain time, it won't be like that at camp. We're graduating in June, and our parents are going to be giving us more freedom to set our own guidelines and boundaries. We could easily drive down to the river at eight o'clock, planning to be there for an hour or so, but then staying until midnight. And four hours of kissing you after not seeing you all week, and knowing it will be a week before I have time with you again—that has disaster written all over it.

(Big Sigh) So, anyway, that's what I have to say, and I hope you understand. We can talk about it more, and I do want you to be honest about how you feel. I don't want you to say it's fine if it's not; number one because I always want us to make decisions together based on what we both need and feel would be best for us, and number two because if you're not committed to it with me and we don't come up with an alternate plan, then I know one night I'm going to say, 'I want to kiss you—just once', and you won't try to stop me, and I

*know in that kind of situation, kissing you 'just once' will
be impossible.*

*I love you, Amber. Very, very much. Call me if you
need to. For you, I'm never more than a phone call
away.*

> *Loving you more every day,*
> *Seth*

*Since this is the kind of life we have chosen, the life
of the Spirit, let us make sure that we do not just hold it
as an idea in our heads or a sentiment in our hearts,
but work out its implications in every detail of our lives.*
Galatians 5:25 (THE MESSAGE)

Amber opened the second letter to see if Seth had anything
to add on that subject, but he didn't mention it. His words were
more standard: 'I had a great time with you this weekend, and I
miss you.' Laying the letter aside, she started crying. She had
been thinking about this summer a lot and had similar thoughts
about them being in more danger of going too far physically for
the same reasons Seth had mentioned. She had been trying
not to think about it, telling herself she was concerned about
nothing—that she didn't need to worry about Seth taking things
too far, but deep down she knew he was struggling more now,
and she didn't know what to do about it.

She had cried one night last week when it had been on her
mind, and she had opened her heart to God, sharing her fears
with Him and asking Him to help her with her increasing
feelings of weakness and to help Seth also. She had forgotten
about that until now, but her words came back to her clearly: *I*

need to talk to Seth about this, but I don't know how. Please show me and provide the right opportunity.

Tonight her tears were not ones of uncertainty and fear. They were tears of gratitude. She was reminded once again that God loved her and was always near. She could go to Him about anything and He would be faithful to provide exactly what she needed. He didn't expect her to do this all by herself.

She decided to write a letter to Seth to keep him from unnecessary worry that she was mad at him. She hadn't even thought of his 'no kissing' idea as a solution, but she knew it was perfect and something that would not be easy to stick with, but much easier than trying to stop kissing once they got started.

Those times with him down by the river last summer were some of her sweetest memories. They always talked the best there, and she had felt very close to him. Last summer they had been able to keep their kissing sweet and innocent during that time, but she agreed with Seth. This summer would be different. They were closer emotionally now, and she didn't know why, but that made their kissing more intense and intimate than ever. Even the thought of it stirred up desires within her she didn't know what to do with.

Dear Seth,

Thank you for having the courage to write me that letter. I agree with you one-hundred percent. I had been thinking of talking to you about the same thing, but I didn't know how. I did pray, however, and God took care of it by talking to you first. Big surprise, huh? He's watching over us, Seth. I don't know why I have to keep being reminded of that, but I do, and I don't know why He's so patient with me, but He is.

Another thing I was thinking regarding this summer is I'd like to come home a few more times since we'll be leaving for college at the end of August. I know it's a long drive for only a few hours with my family, but it's worth it to me, and three hours with you in the car each way won't be bad either.

I'm also wondering about what kind of boundaries you're thinking of for when we get to college—and I know you've been thinking about it! Please share your thoughts with me on that. I don't know what kind of policy the school has about curfew, but even if they don't have one, I'd like us to set one for ourselves. Knowing I need to say good-night to you by a certain time has always been a good thing for me, because if it was up to me I'd stay up with you all night.

I can't wait to see you this weekend. And I can't wait for Matt and Mandy to see each other again. I know. I'm hopeless. But I can totally picture them together, can't you? I know you think we should stay out of it, but you may want to let Matt know he has some competition on his hands. If he's having strong feelings for Mandy, he may want to give her some indication of that this weekend.

I'm glad I never had to sit around wondering with you, Seth. You stepped in and invaded my heart without giving me much say in the matter. And I'm glad, because otherwise I would have dismissed you as a great guy I met but would never be mine in a million years, just like Mandy is thinking about Matt. You're everything I never knew I needed until you were there, *and I continue to see that. So don't stop being exactly who you are, because you are exactly who I need.*

Yours for always,
Amber

Chapter Seven

Amber had finished writing her letter to Seth when her mom knocked on the door and let her know dinner was ready. Going downstairs with a light heart, she enjoyed a relaxing dinner with her mom and dad, something she hadn't had much time for lately with her busy softball schedule. She told them about being accepted to camp, and they weren't surprised. She decided to ask them about something she had been wondering.

"Are you going to want to talk to me and Seth like you did last year, or are you trusting us to set our own standards about the time we spend together?"

Her dad answered. "We're trusting you, Jewel, but if you want me to talk to Seth, I will."

She smiled. "I don't think that's necessary, and I do think it's good for us to figure it out for ourselves. We've already talked about it some, but I wanted to make sure you didn't have your own input before we start making decisions."

"Do you mind if we ask what those are?"

She told them about Seth's "no kissing" idea for any alone-time they have together this summer. Her dad stared at her for a moment and then looked at her mom.

"That kid is set on outdoing me, isn't he? He's honest-to-God trying to steal my daughter's heart right from under my nose."

Her mom laughed. "Yes, I believe he is."

Her dad shook his head and went back to eating, and Amber laughed also.

"Sorry, Daddy."

Her dad looked back at her and spoke seriously. "I'm not sorry. I just got what I prayed for."

She told them about wanting to come home a little more this summer also, and they said they could probably come down to the camp if that would be easier. She said she wouldn't mind having that time with Seth on the drive, but they would let them know once the summer came.

After dinner she went upstairs and decided to do her Bible reading. She hadn't been able to this morning. She had a lot of homework tonight, but she knew she needed her time with Jesus, and she didn't rush. She had been enjoying her reading the last several weeks in John 14 and 15 where Jesus was speaking to His disciples about how to have a relationship with God. Some of it was new to her, and some of it she needed to be reminded of.

She got all of her homework done, but she was too tired to study for a test in history she had coming up on Thursday. She didn't know if she would have much time to study tomorrow. They had a softball game at another school, but their game was canceled due to rain, giving her plenty of time to study after a short indoor practice on Wednesday afternoon. She was able to go to youth group for the first time in two weeks and had time to write before she went to bed.

On Thursday evening Seth called her. He had gotten her letter, and he said he couldn't wait two more days to let her know how much he loved her. "I thought I might come out tomorrow night," he said. "Would that be all right with you?"

"I thought you decided to work on Saturday."

"I did, and I'm going to, but I could have a little time with you before your game and then drive you home afterwards."

"And if the game is canceled, we'd have lots of time."

"That's what I was thinking. It's supposed to rain tomorrow."

"You know, two years ago I would have been praying for dry weather."

"And now?" he asked.

"Let it rain, Jesus."

He laughed. "I love you, baby."

"I love you more."

"Not possible."

"Are you ever going to let me win that argument?"

"Nope."

"Have you talked to Matt about what I said?"

"Yes, and you know what he said?"

"What?"

"If Mandy is meant to be mine, it will work out."

She let out a huff. "Since when did he become so spiritual?"

Seth laughed. "Be careful what you pray for."

"I guess so! I have to leave them in God's hands, huh?"

"That's a good place for them to be, sweetheart."

"I know."

They talked for awhile longer and then he told her good night, telling her he would be out after school tomorrow. The game was rained out, and they went to visit Grandma and Mandy instead and then drove to her house for dinner. They spent a quiet evening with her parents, watching a movie, eating ice cream, and kissing in front of the fire when her parents gave them privacy.

"Are you sure you're okay with us not doing much of that this summer?" Seth asked.

"We will gain far more than we give up."

He smiled. "Have you been reading the Bible again?"

"Every day."

"I've really liked these last few weeks," he said. "He commands us to love each other, you know."

She smiled and received another sweet kiss. "Do you know what I learned on Wednesday night at youth group?"

"What?"

"My dad talked about some of the things God commands us to do, and he said in the original languages of the Bible, the word "command" means to urge us to do or not do something, like God is pleading with us: 'Do this and it will be great for you, I promise'; or 'Don't do that. It's not good. I'm warning you.' And when I read the verse about loving each other this morning, I realized we can never go wrong by loving someone. They might not always return our love, but we will be the better for it, and so will they."

He had planned to leave at nine, but the rain was really coming down. Her dad suggested he stay overnight and drive into work in the morning. It was supposed to stop raining sometime in the night and be clearer tomorrow. Seth didn't argue.

"Could I talk to you for a minute, Seth?" her dad asked after Seth had called his mom and dad to let them know his change of plans. "Privately?"

"Sure," Seth said, following him to the front door and stepping outside.

Amber looked at her mom. "What's that about?"

Her mom smiled. "I believe it has something to do with you dating a boy we prayed for but weren't entirely sure existed."

"What's Daddy going to tell him?"

"I don't know for sure, but considering the fact I caught him crying during his prayer time this morning, I expect a 'thank you' will be in there somewhere."

"Daddy was crying? About me?"

64

Her mom nodded. "All I've heard your dad pray over and over for you and Ben is that you would choose God's best for your lives, go wherever He leads, and seek Him with all of your heart; and he sees Seth as a big part of all that happening in you."

After Seth and her dad returned and her parents went upstairs, Amber asked Seth if everything was okay, wanting to make sure there wasn't some kind of a problem.

"I'm a little surprised you told them," he said.

"About what?"

"About us not kissing."

"I guess it's official now, huh?"

"I'm serious about it."

"I know. What did my dad say?"

"He thanked me for being someone he could trust, and he had a few suggestions and insights for when we're at college together based on his own experience with that."

Seth seemed fine with whatever he had said, so she didn't comment.

"He also said Ben has been struggling a bit. Nothing major, just with normal thoughts and desires he's concerned about getting out of hand. Ben asked your dad to pray for him, and he thought I might want to call or talk to Ben the next time he's here."

"Are you going to?"

"I was going to talk to Ben about us anyway, so I told him I would."

Amber felt concerned for her brother and Hope, but she supposed if Ben had talked to Dad about it, that was better than trying to handle it all himself. She had been praying for them more than usual since Hope had said they were discussing something, and she wondered if it had anything to do with that.

"Did Ben talk to you when they were here?"

"Why do you ask?"

"Just wondering."

"Did Ben talk to you?"

"Not about him and Hope."

"He said something to me, but he wanted me to keep it to myself."

"Tell me!"

Seth shook his head. "Sorry, sweetheart. You'll have to get it out of your brother on your own."

"Is it bad?" she asked.

"No, it's not bad. Just something he's thinking about."

Amber didn't like being kept in the dark, but she knew what it was like to be told something in confidence and having to keep it to herself, so she let it drop.

Chapter Eight

Amber didn't know who was more nervous on the ride into Portland on Saturday afternoon: Mandy or herself. Mandy was still not convinced Matt had any interest in her whatsoever, and her mind seemed to be more on the concert than whom they would be going with. Mandy was also excited about seeing Seth's house for the first time and spending the night there.

Amber was excited about seeing Seth and attending the concert, but more than anything she was anxious to see how Matt interacted with Mandy, and what, if anything, he would do to let her know he liked her. She didn't know Matt that well, and if he wanted to take his time with this, she didn't know what that meant exactly, but she hoped he would make the effort to talk to Mandy and not act too aloof around her, or Mandy may be writing a letter to Jeremiah on Monday.

Amber didn't know why she had a special feeling about Matt and Mandy, she just did. She couldn't help it. No matter how many times she told herself to put it out of her mind and wait to see if anything happened, her mind kept returning to the possibilities. Writing a story based on them probably didn't help, but she couldn't seem to help that either. The story just kept rolling along.

Arriving at the MAX station in downtown Portland, they saw Seth waiting on the platform for them. The three of them walked to his car. It was cool outside but not raining.

"How was your tournament?" Seth asked, giving her a hug before opening the car door for her.

"Good. We won both of our games."

"Are you tired?"

"Not really," she said. Mandy had already gotten into the car, and she whispered, "I'm too excited to be tired."

He laughed at her and opened the door. They drove to the church. The vans were leaving at five. The concert was in Salem, about an hour away, and they were planning to have dinner when they got there. They hung out with the others in the parking lot while waiting for everyone to arrive. Amber spotted Matt coming from the side door of the church. He walked toward them, and Amber found herself holding her breath.

"Did you have band rehearsal this afternoon?" Seth asked him.

"Yep. We usually have it later but since most of us were going to the concert, we moved it up." In almost the same breath Matt turned toward her and Mandy and said hello to both of them.

They returned the greeting, and Amber gave him a hug. "Good to see you," she said. She caught the nice scent of his cologne and could feel his heart beating rapidly through his shirt.

"Good to see you too," he replied. "This guy treating you all right?"

She smiled. "Always."

"Good to see you too, Mandy," Matt said. "How are you?"

"Fine, thanks," she said. "How are you?"

"Good," he replied and then added, "Would you like to see that keyboard I was telling you about? It's all set up for tomorrow right now."

"Sure," she said. "I'd love to."

Very smooth, Matt. He had obviously already learned about Mandy's piano talents. If there was one quick way into Mandy's heart, it was her love of music.

The two of them walked toward the church together, and Amber stood there in shock that Matt had actually made a move. Seth smiled at her and stepped closer.

"I can't believe he did that," Seth echoed her thoughts. "He didn't even look nervous."

"He's nervous," Amber assured him. "His heart is going a mile a minute."

Seth laughed and corralled her into a playful hug. "Is that why girls are always hugging guys, to see how fast their heart is beating for them?"

She laughed. "I don't think so. I didn't think about him being nervous until I felt it, but it would have been very difficult to miss."

The vans began to load up before Matt and Mandy returned. Amber and Seth found some seats and saved two behind them, giving Matt and Mandy little choice about sitting together when they arrived.

"Do you need to sit up front?" Amber asked her.

"Not if it's mostly freeway," she said. "Is it?"

"Yes," Seth replied.

Mandy took the seat by the window and Matt sat beside her. "Do you get carsick easy?" he asked.

"Yes. But only on winding roads. I'll be fine."

He leaned over and whispered something in her ear Amber couldn't hear, and Mandy smiled at him but didn't reply. Amber turned around and resisted the urge to watch. Seth was leaning against the window and could talk to Matt easily, but he gave them their own space about twenty minutes into the trip. He pulled her close to his side, and whispered in her ear.

"He is so gone on her."

Once they got to Salem, the vans stopped at a pizza place, and they all went inside for dinner. The four of them sat together, along with Kerri and Dylan who were still close friends. Kerri had told Dylan she didn't feel it was meant to be for them on a long-term basis, and Dylan had respected her decision, but Amber thought he seemed to be looking at Kerri the same as always.

When the guys went to play video games and Kerri left to use the restroom, Amber had a chance to talk to Mandy alone. "You two seem to have a lot to talk about," she said.

Mandy smiled. "I don't know why, but I can talk to him about anything. That's so not like me!"

"He likes you," Amber said, feeling she could say so based on what she had seen tonight, not because she had inside information.

"You think so? Isn't he that way with everybody?"

"Yes, but he's going out of his way to talk to you and ignoring everyone else—even Seth. That's not just him being friendly. Trust me."

"What am I supposed to do?"

"What you've been doing. Be yourself, Mandy. I've never seen you doing anything else with him. Don't try to fix what isn't broken."

The rest of the evening went pretty much the same. They sat together in their same spots on the short drive to the concert, and the six of them found seats together in the church auditorium to listen to Bethany Dillon and the opening bands perform. On the drive home Amber fell asleep on Seth's shoulder with Matt and Mandy sitting behind them.

Returning to the church, she and Seth, along with Mandy and Kerri walked to Seth's car. Both Dylan and Matt followed them to say good night. Dylan did so rather briefly, but Matt lingered a bit longer.

"Will you be at church tomorrow?" Matt asked Mandy before she got inside the car.

"Yes, I think so."

"Okay, I'll see you then."

"Okay," she said in her beautifully sweet way that Amber admired and envied. She often wished she was more soft-spoken like that.

Once they were headed toward the house, Kerri said something blunt. Amber knew she spoke purely out of what she had observed tonight. Seth hadn't told his sister anything as far as Amber knew, and she didn't think Kerri would say it if she knew Matt's interest in Mandy was supposed to be a secret.

"I think Matthew has a crush on someone."

Amber was in the back with Kerri. The roads to Seth's house were curvy and she didn't want Mandy getting sick on the short drive. She leaned forward and spoke to Mandy, but loudly enough for them all to hear. "Told you so."

"You guys, stop," Mandy said, sounding embarrassed but not denying their words.

Amber sat back and decided to be good. If Seth or Kerri wanted to add anything, she thought that would be good for her cousin's self-esteem, but if she did it, she would embarrass her.

"I've known Matt a long time, Mandy," Kerri said, not letting the subject drop, "and I've never seen him like that. Right, Seth?"

"He seemed rather attentive," he said.

"Rather attentive! More like, 'Hello, Matt. There are forty other people here, not just Amber's sweet cousin.'"

Kerri didn't say anything else, but Amber hoped it was enough to convince Mandy that Matt was interested in her. The two of them slept in Kerri's room, and Kerri slept on the couch downstairs, so they stayed up late talking.

"I do like him, and if he likes me back, I'd be happy to hear that from him, but I'm not sure I want to start something with him or anyone right now. This summer is going to be weird, being back with my old friends I might never see again, and then heading off to college in the fall. I'd almost prefer to wait until then, you know?"

"Yeah, I understand. And it's not like you'll be short on time once September comes. Four years is a long time for anything to happen."

"Unless he ends up getting together with someone else before then. If he doesn't, it would be ideal, but if he does, I might never get my chance."

"Then you need to let him know how you honestly feel. I think Matt will wait until September if he knows you're interested, but if he doesn't, then he might not think he has any reason to."

"What am I supposed to do? Corner him tomorrow and say, 'I'm not ready yet, but wait for me. I'll be yours in California.'?"

"Sounds good to me."

"Yeah, right. Like I'm ever going to do that."

"He might be going to the beach in two weeks. You could see him again then, and you never know, he might actually tell you how he feels, and then you can tell him what you just told me."

Mandy appeared mildly hopeful about that. "You know what I like best about him?"

"What?"

"He makes me smile."

"That's an important thing," she replied. "Take it from a girl whose boyfriend makes her smile all the time—even in embarrassing and difficult moments."

"He told me I had a nice smile."

"He did? When?"

"When he was showing me the keyboard at the church. I couldn't stop smiling because it was so nice, and when he asked me if I liked it, I said, 'Can't you tell? I can't stop smiling!' And then he said it. He's so—" She searched for the right word.

"Honest?"

"Yes," she agreed. "But not like he says whatever he's thinking. He doesn't hold back, but he waits for the right moment. If he would have said that at any other time, I would have been embarrassed and seen it as him being flirty. But having him go from telling me about the keyboard to saying, 'And you have a beautiful smile.' It made me want to be kissed."

Amber smiled. She knew what Mandy meant, remembering the first time she felt that way about Seth. "I know I keep saying this, but be yourself, Mandy. That's all I've ever seen you do around Matt, and I think he likes what he sees. I don't think you need to force anything. When the time is right, it will happen."

Amber had come to a place in her story inspired by Matt and Mandy where she wasn't sure where to take it next. She was thinking about it after she turned out the light, and she was tempted to write what she wanted to happen, but she decided to wait and see what happened in real life, and then she would write it that way. She was doing so with Stacey and Kenny's story, but it was easier because everything had already happened. With Matt and Mandy, however, she was going to have to wait and see.

Chapter Nine

Amber felt nervous about seeing Seth in the morning. She had given him her laptop before they went to bed, telling him he could read some of her story about Stacey and Kenny. They had gotten back late from the concert, and she didn't know if he had read any before he went to sleep or if he planned to wait until sometime today.

She knew the writing itself was good, simply because she wrote like she always did, and he had always complimented her writing in the past. But being able to develop a complete novel that was worth reading was a different thing entirely. The story wasn't super-dramatic with all kinds of crazy or tragic things happening to the main character, like in some books she'd read. It was about everyday life as a teenager: school, family, relationships with friends, and this girl's first long-term dating experience.

But it was real. It was Stacey's life with some minor differences. Anyone who knew Stacey would likely see the similarities, and yet it was fictionalized because she didn't know every detail. She wanted Seth to be honest with her, and she knew he likely would be—something she hoped for and dreaded at the same time.

When she and Mandy arrived downstairs for a light breakfast before they headed to church, Seth was waiting for her inside the kitchen doorway. He told Mandy to go ahead and sit at the table with Kerri and help herself to the cereal and fruit, but he pulled her away into the den beyond the kitchen that overlooked the valley and hillsides in the distance.

She thought this must have something to do with Matt, that he had texted Seth last night or this morning and told him he was planning to talk to Mandy about the way he felt, like she had imagined him doing as one of her future-scenes in her story. But this wasn't about Matt and Mandy, it was about her.

"I read your story," he said. "I was up until two a.m., and then I read the rest of it this morning."

"You read all of it?"

"Yes."

It wasn't finished. She supposed she was about two-thirds of the way done, but still, that was a lot for him to read.

"What do you think?" she asked.

"I think it's great."

"Really?"

He smiled and pulled her into a warm hug. "It's very good, sweetheart. I mean it. You have a gift."

Amber felt something she did not expect. She appreciated Seth's praise, and it made her feel good, but beyond that she felt God laying a familiar calling on her heart. She had felt God leading her to write these kinds of stories, but she didn't know if she could actually do it. But now she did. She could write books, good books, and God could use them to touch the lives of others.

The thought overwhelmed her, and she started crying. Seth held her close and didn't say anything. But he did kiss her in a tender and affectionate way. She knew he believed in her and would support her in this. And that meant the world to her.

Matt talked to Mandy at church, much the same way as he had yesterday, and Amber watched and enjoyed the special look Matt brought to her cousin's face. The four of them spent the afternoon together, and when Seth dropped Matt off at his house, Matt told Mandy good-bye and asked if she was going to the beach with them in two weeks.

"Yes, I think so," she said.

"See you then," he said to Mandy specifically before saying good-bye to her and Seth also.

Once they were on the train headed for home, Amber didn't tease Mandy about it. Mandy didn't say anything about writing a letter to either Matt or Jeremiah, and Amber didn't ask. She had a feeling Mandy wouldn't write to either one. Mandy had enough to hope for with Matt and would likely wait to see what happened in two weeks when she had the chance to see him again.

When Amber got home she checked her email and had a message waiting for her from Seth. It was titled: **He makes me smile.**

Hi, sweetheart. This message from Paige was waiting for me when I got home, and I knew you would want to read it too. We have an amazing God. He makes me smile.

Dear Seth,

You've probably wondered what happened to me. I've been thinking about what you said all week, and I even prayed a few times, asking God to show me if he's real or not. I wasn't sure if that was an okay thing to pray for, but I did anyway, and now I think it's okay because he did it this morning!

I decided to go to church. I live just down the street from this big one that I know a lot of kids go to, and

I decided to give it a try, figuring I could slip in without anyone noticing me and check it out. So I went by myself, but practically the first person I saw after I walked in the door was my English teacher, Mrs. Evans! She was my teacher last year and also for Creative Writing that I took with Amber last semester. She asked me if I had come with anyone, and when I said no, she invited me to sit with her and her family.

It was strange. I felt like I didn't belong there, and yet I did. I felt like God was all around me, and yet it wasn't the first time I had encountered him. I mostly watched and listened—to the music and people who spoke, and to those around me. By the end I knew I had experienced God in a way I couldn't explain but I knew was real. The pastor talked about that verse you sent me in your last email—the one about not conforming to this world but being transformed by God and changing the way we think. I realized I've been following the masses—doing what my friends do and living like people on TV and in the movies, but it's not working. I'm so messed up and not even happy most of the time.

Afterwards Mrs. Evans invited me out to lunch and we went, just her and me, and I ended up telling her about you and what you had told me and how I'd been thinking about it all week. When she drove me home, she said if I ever wanted to talk she was available to listen, and before I got out of the car I told her I didn't want to let the opportunity to know

God slip by. She offered to pray with me, and I told God everything I was thinking and feeling. I asked him to help me to know him and be in my life. As soon as I spoke the words I felt so different, like I was suddenly a new person with a whole new life!!!

Something tells me I'm going to have to completely change my life. And I feel like I want to tell everyone what happened, but I'm not sure how. It's not like people can see inside my heart and know it's different. I guess I'll have to show them with my life—with the changes I make, right? I think I'm going to be watching Amber more closely and see how she lives. I want to be like her. Do you think that's possible? I've made so many mistakes already that I know she's never made. I'd like to hear your thoughts on that.

Thanks for telling me about God, Seth. I think you'll be good at that youth ministry thing. If you can help me understand, you can help anybody!!!

Paige

Amber knew she shouldn't be amazed by what God had done, but she was. And she knew only He could have done that. She almost called Stacey to tell her, but she decided to wait until she saw her at Bible study tonight so she could see her face, and the wait was worth it.

"You're not serious," she said, honestly appearing to not believe her.

"Yes. I am."

"You're talking about Paige Gibson?"

"Yes," she laughed. "Can you believe it? Isn't that cool?"

"Yes, it is cool, and no, I can't believe it."

"Well, believe it, Stace, and be prepared to talk to her about it because I know she needs someone like you who can relate to getting to know God at this point in her life."

"She doesn't even know I'm a Christian, Amber. We've never talked about it."

"So? Tell her now. She needs a friend in this, and you're the best candidate. Tell her about the difference God has made in your life and that He can do the same for her."

Stacey didn't have to wait long for her chance to talk to Paige. The following afternoon they had a softball game at St. Mary's in Portland, and Amber saw Stacey talking to her on the way there, and once they got to the school and were warming up, Stacey confirmed they'd had a good talk. Amber had a chance to say something to Paige herself while they were both waiting for their turn to bat. All she said was, "I'm really happy for you, Paige."

Paige knew what she meant and turned to give her a hug. Neither of them said anything else. After the game she went to say good-bye to Seth and thanked him for coming to watch her play. He walked with her to the bus, and Paige saw him then, stepping over to say 'hi'.

"Hey, Paige," he said, not hesitating to give her a hug, which she seemed a little caught off-guard by. She started crying and couldn't speak with more than a whisper.

"It's a whole new life," she said. "Thank you."

She smiled at them both and then turned to get on the bus. Amber stepped into Seth's arms and said, "I think you're pretty incredible."

"We're a team, Amber. You and me. God used us both."

Paige sat with Stacey on the ride home, and Amber continued to pray for Paige, and for Stacey, that God would give her the words Paige needed to hear. When they returned to the school, Amber met up with Stacey, and before they left, Paige said something to them.

"Does this feeling ever go away?"

"What feeling?" Amber asked.

"The feeling of being completely free and, I don't know, at peace, I guess."

"Only if you let it," Amber said. "I sometimes let things get in the way of the peace and the joy, but it doesn't have to be that way."

"What gets in the way?"

Stacey answered this time, obviously speaking from experience. "When you stop believing He loves you, when you do things you know aren't right, and when you try to do things on your own instead of trusting Him to help."

Paige spoke again. "This morning I got up and said to God, 'Help me to know you better and live this day the right way.' Do you think I should do that every morning?"

Amber smiled. "I think we all should. Did it work?"

Paige thought for a moment. "Yeah, I guess it did. I wasn't planning to tell anyone, but I ended up telling two people, and then I found out one of my best friends already knows Him and can help me do the same."

"Sounds like a good day," Amber said.

"It was," she laughed. "Good night, you guys. See you tomorrow."

Chapter Ten

"How are you, Nikki?" Amber asked her friend the following Wednesday, letting Nicole know she was looking for a real answer. Since basketball season had ended, she hadn't seen her much except on Sundays because Nikki only had classes in the morning and then went to work in the afternoons, or to volunteer at the pregnancy center. Today she had the day off, so she had hung around for lunch.

Nicole smiled at her. "I am doing very well, Amber."

"You sound sure about that."

"I'm enjoying my less busy schedule this semester, and I'm looking forward to Spencer being home in another six weeks."

"Have you decided what college you're going to?"

"Not yet. I can't decide if I want to be at U of O with Spencer or go to a Christian college. I was almost set on going to George Fox because I know I could really use the God-centeredness of a Christian school, but then I was talking to Spencer about it, and he was telling me about the great on-campus ministry he and Sarah are a part of, and I can see how letting God use me to share the truth in a secular environment could be good too."

"But you'd be all right with being away from Spencer?"

"Yes. Being away from him is actually good for me. When he's around, I become clingy and jealous of his time. I shut out other people more, and God. I hope there will come a day when I can be with him and not be that way, but I need to learn to go to God first—get in the habit of it, you know? And I'm not there yet."

Amber smiled. She had never heard Nikki talk like this or seem so at peace. She truly was a different person than she had been at the beginning of their junior year when she wouldn't even speak to her, and she had made significant progress since the beginning of this year.

"What are your plans for the summer?" Amber asked.

"Spending as much time with Spencer as possible."

She laughed. "Are you both going to be working?"

"Yes, but I told Spencer it's not going to be like last summer. I deliberately agreed to work hours that cut into our time because I was trying to pull away from him and convince myself I needed to let him go. But I'm intending to enjoy every minute we have together. There's a part of me that still doesn't believe he loves me, and I'm planning to let him convince me of that."

"Good for you," Amber spoke seriously. "And you have every reason to believe that, Nikki. He is in love with you. I can see it. Seth does too."

Nicole smiled. "What's this I hear about Paige being at Bible study on Sunday night? Stacey said Seth talked to her about God, and now she's suddenly a Christian?"

Amber smiled. "Yep, that's pretty much it. Wild, huh?"

"When did she talk to him?"

"It was actually through email. Paige met him after one of our softball games last month, and he said some things that made her curious about God, and then Seth followed up with a couple of emails, and it was enough to get her to go to church and believe God loves her and can make a difference in her life."

"And let me guess, she's going to camp this summer and to California with the rest of you now too?"

Amber laughed. "No. She's going to OSU with Stacey, and they're going to be roommates."

"Are you and Seth going to Prom this weekend?"

"No. We decided not to this year. Seth's youth group is going to the beach on Saturday, and we're going there instead. What are you doing this weekend?"

"Seeing my dad. He's coming on Friday. I haven't seen him for almost a month, so I'm really looking forward to it. Did I tell you my mom decided to sell the house?"

"No. When?"

"She's going to put it on the market in a few weeks."

"How do you feel about that?"

"I'm not surprised. She never liked that house."

"You're kidding me. What's not to like?"

"My dad picked it out."

Amber thought for a moment and asked her something. "What do you think happened to them? Or do you know?"

"Honestly, I don't think my mom ever loved him."

"What makes you say that?"

"I always used to think they just didn't get along, but now that I've had all this time to spend with them separately, I've realized that my mom is never happy. She wasn't happy with him, and she's not happy without him. And she's a miserable person to live with. I love her, but no matter what I do, she's never satisfied. She was the same way with my dad. He put up with it for a long time because I think he really did love her, but he couldn't do it anymore, and I don't blame him."

"Why would your mom marry someone she didn't love?"

"Daddy was her ticket to a different life."

"What do you mean?"

"I didn't know this until about six months ago, but I was talking to my dad when I spent some time with him at Christmas. I told him about why I had ended things with

85

Spencer but that we were back together because I had really missed him and realized how much I loved him. He told me he was glad I knew that, and I asked him what he meant. He said my mom had confused love with a better situation; She had been in and out of a bunch of different relationships with guys who didn't treat her well, and so when my dad came along—a good Christian boy who actually treated her with respect, she fell in love with that—but not him, at least that's the way he sees it.

"My dad loved her," Nikki continued, "and she'd never had that before, but her wounds went too deep, and she needed more than a nice boyfriend to heal her. She needed God, but according to my dad, she never came to Him fully. She went through the motions. She went to church after they got married, but it was never personal for her. It was just something they did. I've tried talking to her since I learned that, but she doesn't want to listen. Apparently my dad tried to talk to her about it for a long time too, but she could never see it. She could never see God's love. She could never get beyond the pain she'd experienced. I think she married my dad, thinking that would heal all of her hurts, but he couldn't do that. And I understand, because even with as forgiving as Spencer was with me after I begged him to have sex with me, it wasn't until I went to Jesus that I truly found what I needed. And it's not a one-time thing. I have to keep going back, find my healing and security in Him, and then I can let Spencer love me."

Amber remembered having a similar conversation with Hope back when she and Ben were first dating, and Amber decided to call her the following evening. After they talked for awhile, she told Hope about talking to Nikki, and she asked how she was doing with that.

"Every once in awhile I start to feel like I have no business being with Ben, but I can never stay there for long because

Jesus is faithful to remind me I'm not the person I used to be. I know He has healed me and restored me and I'm free to love Ben and be loved by him."

"Not that I think this about you," Amber said, "but did you ever just see Ben as something better than what you'd had before?"

"I spent the first four months of our relationship trying to figure that out. The last thing I wanted to do was hurt Ben, and once he convinced me he really did like me just for who I was, I wanted to make sure I felt the same way about him."

"Was there something specific that made you feel that way, or was it a gradual thing?"

"No, there was something specific."

"What?"

"When he kissed me."

Amber laughed. "That good, huh?"

"It was amazing. They're still amazing. When Ben kisses me, he touches something deep in my heart—like he's not just kissing my lips but my soul. Do you know what I mean?"

"Yes. I know what you mean," she said.

They were both silent for a moment, and then Hope said, "Can I tell you something?"

"Sure."

"Can you keep a secret?"

"From who?"

"Your mom and dad."

"Okay."

"You know how I told you that Ben and I have been discussing something?"

"Yes."

"Ben wanted to keep this between us, but only because he doesn't want me to feel pressured, and I feel like I need to hear what you think."

"What's going on?"

"He asked me to marry him."

Amber gasped. "When?"

"On my birthday. He wants us to get married either in September before school starts, or in December during Winter Break."

Amber smiled. "What did you tell him?"

"He told me I could take time to think about it, so I didn't tell him anything at first. He tells me almost every day he's serious, and I believe it, but it's been three weeks now, and I can't make up my mind. I know I love him, but I'm not sure if I'm ready for that."

"What do you want, Hope? Not, what do you think you should do, but what do you want? You have to know that."

Hope sighed, and Amber knew what she was going to say.

"I want to get married."

"When?"

"Around Christmas. That will be two years since we first met and two years since I've truly felt healed."

"Then tell Ben that."

"You know what I was doing right before you called?"

"What?"

"Lexi is studying with Josh tonight, and I was just lying here praying, asking God what I was supposed to do. I've been praying all along, but tonight I was at the end of myself—weary of trying to figure out what's right."

"It's been awhile since I've felt the need to call you."

"And you didn't know anything about this?"

"No."

"Seth didn't tell you?"

"Seth? How would he know?"

"Ben told him."

"He did? Why?"

"It sort of spilled out when we saw you guys that weekend. He said he asked Seth not to say anything to you."

"And he didn't," she laughed but then remembered something. "Oh wait, he did say Ben had told him something he couldn't tell me. I never thought about it being that."

"You know why I think Ben asked me?"

"Why?"

"The night Seth called him and asked if he knew anything about why you were breaking up with him, Ben called me and said, 'Do you love me?' And I said, 'Yes,' not knowing anything about him talking to Seth. And then he said, 'If you were going to break up with me, how would you do it?' And I told him I didn't know because I'd never thought about it, and then he told me about talking to Seth, and it was the first time I ever heard Ben sounding worried I was going to do something like that to him. And it really hit me how much he loves me, and you know what I said?"

"What?"

"'I love you, Ben, and I want you for the rest of my life if you'll have me.'"

Amber smiled. "So you really proposed to him first."

"Yeah, I guess I did," she laughed. "Maybe when I see him tomorrow night I'll ask him if he's made up his mind yet."

Amber laughed. "You should. Let me know what he says."

"I will."

"I love you, Hope. Are you still coming home for a visit next weekend?"

"We were planning on it, and we definitely will be now. Ben has to talk to my daddy before this can be official."

"Okay. I'll look forward to seeing you both."

"Us too. Love you, honey. Thanks for talking."

"Anytime, sis."

"Okay, now you're going to make me cry."

She let her go and decided to call Seth.

"Hi, sweetheart. Everything all right?"

"Yes. Guess what?"

"What?"

"Guess!"

He laughed. "I have no idea."

"Yes you do. What good news would you be expecting me to hear any day?"

He hesitated but went ahead and said it. "Hope said yes?"

"Yes! Well, she's planning to. I just talked to her."

"Are you mad?"

"Am I mad?"

"That I didn't tell you?"

"Not if Ben asked you not to."

"How did you find out?"

"I called Hope, just to talk, and she told me. She asked for my advice."

"Then she must have been ready to say yes," he laughed.

"Yes, I think she was."

"Did I tell you my boss is getting married?"

"No. When?"

"In two weeks."

"His first wife died, right?"

"Yes. Several years ago. He wasn't sure if he would ever want to marry someone else, but I guess the right woman came along."

They talked for a long time, much longer than they usually allowed themselves on a school night. They both had spring-fever and were beyond caring about getting all of their homework done, although Seth said he was basically finished. She wasn't, but she felt too excited about Ben and Hope to do any.

"Has Matt said anything to you about Saturday?"

"Yes. He's looking forward to it. Is Mandy still coming?"

"As far as I know."

"Did she talk to you more about her time with him at the concert?"

"Not really. I think she wants Matt to like her, but she's afraid of it at the same time."

"Is that the way you felt about me?"

"Absolutely."

"What is it with you wonderful, dream-come-true girls never thinking you're good enough for us good-looking but mostly idiotic guys?"

"Oh, please. You're hardly idiotic."

"We're idiots. Trust me. It took me seven days to let you know how I felt about you. It's only by God's grace that someone didn't get to you before I did."

"Lucky for you, you have that."

"And He knew exactly who I needed, Amber Kristine Wilson."

She laughed. "A.K.A. Kit Kat."

"A.K.A. Sweetheart."

"A.K.A. Your incredibly blessed girlfriend."

He was silent for a moment and then said something that melted her heart and left her absolutely speechless.

"Also known as: The girl I fall more in love with every day and want to spend the rest of my life with."

She let those words sink deep into her heart, and she felt a desire for something she had thought of often but had never desired fully until this moment. She wanted to marry Seth—perhaps much sooner than she had seriously considered before, and that took her by surprise.

Seth responded to her silence. "I mean it, Amber. I'm not joking about that."

"I know," she whispered. "And I'm glad because that's what I want too."

"Is it?"

"Yes."

"We could get married at Christmas too."

She knew he wasn't kidding. If he would have said that forty-five minutes ago when she told him about Ben and Hope, she would have laughed and not taken him seriously. But this conversation, and her heart, had taken a sudden new path. A path she wasn't afraid of and wanted to explore a little bit.

"You know my boss, Mr. Davidson?"

"Yes."

"He married his first wife when they were eighteen. I've asked him before if he ever regretted that or felt like they'd rushed into it, and he said, 'That would have been less years we would have had together. Life is short, Seth. You can't always count on tomorrow.'"

Seth didn't push it further, but she knew this wasn't the end of this conversation. His silence didn't tell her he regretted his words, but that he was doing some serious thinking and allowing her to do the same.

"I hate to say this, but I should probably go and get a little homework done here," she said.

"Okay. I suppose I can pull myself away since I'll be seeing you less than twenty-four hours from now."

"I can't wait," she said.

"I love you, Amber. I didn't say anything tonight I didn't mean."

"I know you didn't."

"Are you okay, or did I scare you?"

She smiled. "I'm very okay, Seth. I love you."

"I love you too. Good night, baby."

"Good night."

Chapter Eleven

"I'm not going, Amber."

"What? Why not?"

"Because," Mandy whined. "I feel like I'm only going to see Matt."

"So? What's wrong with that?"

"What if he sees me and thinks, 'Oh, great. She's here too? Now I'm going to have to hang around her and act like I'm enjoying myself.'?"

Amber laughed.

"I'm serious, Amber!"

"I know you are," she said. "I'm not laughing at you. I'm laughing at me. I remember thinking the exact same thing about inviting Seth to my birthday party. After I did, I kept imagining him getting my message and thinking, 'Oh, great. She invited me to her party. Now I'm going to have to act like I was serious about wanting to see her again sometime.'"

"But that's different," Mandy insisted. "Seth had already told you he liked you."

"Only because he knew if he didn't say anything he might never see me again."

Mandy didn't look convinced. She seemed to have lost her hope and confidence from the night of the concert two weeks ago. Amber added something she knew to be the absolute truth. "If you're not there tomorrow, I think Matt will be disappointed, and then you really will be ruining his day."

Mandy finished packing her bag, and they left from their grandmother's house for her softball game. Seth was waiting for them in the parking area outside the field, but he wasn't alone as she expected him to be. Kerri and Matt were with him.

"Hey, guys," she said, giving Kerri a hug. "What are you doing here?"

"I've been meaning to come watch you play," Kerri said. "And since our senior year is about up, I decided I'd better get out here."

"That's sweet of you. I hope I don't disappoint you. This is a tough team we're playing tonight."

"It will be fun either way," she said.

Amber turned to greet Matt also, but his eyes were already elsewhere. She didn't interfere.

"Hi, Mandy," he said. "I heard you might be here tonight."

"I am," she said, giving him her best smile.

Amber turned her attention to Seth and gave him a hug. Her thoughts were heavily on Mandy and how she was taking Matt's unexpected presence here, but as soon as Seth spoke soft words in her ear, her mind took a detour, remembering their conversation from last night.

"I've been thinking about you all day."

She held on to him and enjoyed the private moment in the middle of their group of friends. He held her close to him, and there wasn't a doubt in her mind he was thinking the same thing she was. "I've been thinking about you too," she said.

They headed for the field, and he gave her a kiss before she went to warm up with Stacey. Somehow she managed to pitch and play well throughout the long game that ended up being closer than she expected it to be against Reynolds, the second-place team in their league behind Centennial. In the final inning Paige hit a triple with two girls on base to put them ahead by one run.

Heading for the pitcher's mound for the bottom of the ninth where Amber knew she had her work cut out for her, she realized how much her mind had not been on this game, which wasn't like her at all. She was usually very focused, but tonight she had allowed ten years of experience to take over while her heart and mind were in another world. A world where she was completely in love with Seth and had a strong desire to spend the rest of her life with him—something she had known would likely happen sometime in the future, but now? She was pleasantly surprised and couldn't keep the corners of her lips from rising as she waited for the first batter to come to the plate.

She pitched a perfect inning, three batters and three outs. After she threw the final pitch that secured the victory for them, she remained in place and let Stacey and her other teammates come to her. Stacey hugged her first, and most of her teammates took their turn, and it wasn't until then she realized they all saw her as the most valuable player of the game. She had been thinking about the awesome hits others had made, not so much her pitching that held their tough opponents to four hits and two runs.

"What got into you?" her dad said, lifting her off the ground and spinning her around. She smiled and didn't say anything. Even with pulling off a great victory, she continued to have Seth at the forefront of her mind.

He was more patient than everyone else, waiting for her to come meet him. Even Mandy and Kerri came out to give her hugs as she approached them standing at the edge of the field.

"Nice game, Amber," Matt said. He had remained with Seth. "I had no idea. Seth doesn't brag on you nearly enough."

Amber was completely amazed by the way she felt. For years she had been dreaming of a night like this on the softball field. She had pitched nice games before, but never this well against such a strong team, and yet now that she had, it was the furthest thing from her mind. She'd pitched a good game. So what? What did that matter in the overall scheme of her life? What mattered were the people she shared her life with— her teammates, her family and friends, and especially the incredibly great guy who had been consuming her heart and mind all day.

She wasn't the least bit surprised when the first words out of his mouth were not, 'Great game, sweetheart,' as he often said, but rather something no one would find significant except them.

"I love you, baby," he said, holding her close to him as the rest of the world faded away.

"I love you," she said, letting the tears fall. Her teammates had been crying since they had first come to meet her on the pitcher's mound, but she had saved hers until now.

Seth held her for a long time and kept her close to his side as they walked to the car where she said good-bye to her parents. She and Mandy had planned to go home with Seth tonight. The church vans were leaving for the beach at nine tomorrow morning. Since Matt and Kerri had come also, he asked if one of them would like to drive, and Matt said he would. She and Seth sat in the back along with Kerri, who insisted Mandy take the front seat because she tended to get carsick.

Matt and Mandy talked off and on throughout the drive, and Amber had the feeling they had talked quite a bit during the game also. But she was only vaguely aware of anyone but Seth. Once they reached the freeway heading toward Portland, she closed her eyes and pretended to fall asleep against him, simply so she wouldn't have to do or think about anything besides being in the comfort of his arms.

When Matt pulled into the driveway, they all got out of the car, and Seth invited Matt to stay. They headed for the front door. The others stepped inside, but Seth kept her on the porch. He kissed her, and just when she thought maybe she was being too clingy and making too much of his words last night, he kissed her earlobe lightly and whispered in her ear, "You're doing things to my heart, Amber."

She smiled. "I'm doing things? You're the one who brought it up."

"Yes, but you're the one who was in my dreams all night long."

She left that one alone and received another warm and soft kiss. When they went inside, the five of them watched a movie together, and it wasn't until after she and Mandy went upstairs and were alone in Kerri's room that she heard how the evening had gone from her cousin's perspective.

"Did you know he was going to be here?" Mandy asked her.

"No, I didn't. I promise. Were you okay?"

Mandy smiled. "Yes. How does he do that? I panicked when I first saw him but when Seth and Kerri left us alone together before the game started, I was totally fine."

"Why did they leave you alone?"

"They went to get food and drinks from the concession stand. Matt gave Seth money and said, "Here's some for Mandy and me.""

"What did you say?"

"I didn't say anything."

"What did you talk about while they were gone?"

"School mostly. He asked me what I was planning to study at Lifegate, and I told him I wasn't sure but I'm thinking of teaching—probably Language Arts, and he said, 'You'd be the prettiest English teacher I've ever seen.'"

Amber stared at her. If Mandy wasn't getting how much Matt liked her by this point, Amber doubted anything she could say would convince her.

"Do you think he's just being a flirt?" Mandy asked.

"No, Mandy. I don't. I know him better than that."

The following day was more of the same between Matt and Mandy, and herself and Seth. The four of them hung out together most of the day. Matt didn't do anything obvious like hold Mandy's hand, but they all knew exactly what was going on. Matt was wooing Mandy in a slow and steady way and doing exactly what he had told Seth he wanted to do: get to know her in an unofficial but intentional way that allowed Mandy to be herself and get to know him equally well.

After lunch the four of them headed for the sandy beach and took a long walk on the beautiful day. It was sunny and not at all windy. The four of them started out walking side by side, but eventually she and Seth took the lead and let Matt and Mandy follow behind. Amber had enjoyed watching them together. Matt talked almost constantly, and Mandy was more quiet, and yet both of them seemed comfortable being who they were.

Amber wasn't feeling quite as clingy to Seth as she had been last night, but she had a warm feeling in her heart and felt closer to him than ever. She was walking by his side, enjoying the peaceful moment and wondering what Matt and Mandy were talking about when Seth suddenly stopped.

"What?" she asked, looking up at him.

He motioned to something ahead of them. Amber saw two people kissing along the water's edge. It took her a moment to realize it was Kerri and Dylan.

"I thought they broke up," she whispered.

Seth turned them around and headed in the other direction. "Yeah, me too."

Neither of them said anything to Matt and Mandy and let them assume they were ready to head back. Seth glanced over his shoulder, and his words told her this wasn't a brief kiss by any means.

"My sister is going to have some explaining to do later, that's for sure."

Amber laughed. She rarely saw Seth looking so curious, confused, and delighted at the same time. Amber knew Seth liked Dylan and had been a little disappointed when Kerri let him go so easily. He supported her decision, but privately he had told her his personal feelings on the matter.

"Did you ever say anything to him?" she asked, knowing Seth had thought about talking to Dylan and encouraging him to not give up too soon.

"No. I decided to stay out of it."

"Wasn't Dylan pretty adamant about not kissing her unless they both saw this going somewhere?"

"Yep. And Kerri knows that."

Amber thought about her own feelings toward Seth that seemed to have gone to a new level overnight, and she supposed the same thing could have happened to Kerri, just in a different way.

"Sometimes we suddenly see things differently, huh?"

He smiled at her, knowing exactly what she meant. "Do you really think you could marry me by December?"

"A week ago I would have said no, but now I'm not so sure. The thought makes me smile. I know that."

"Me too," he said. "I think we should both pray about it for a few weeks and then talk about it some more, okay?"

"Okay," she said, feeling at peace with that plan. She hadn't asked for these new feelings, and she believed if God was the one who had put them there, He would show her exactly what they meant and what to do about them.

They didn't see Kerri and Dylan again until dinner. The entire group met at a pizza place, planning to head back to

Portland after they ate. Kerri and Dylan came to sit by them and weren't being super-obvious they were together as more than friends, but since she and Seth had seen them kissing earlier, they both noticed when Kerri leaned over and whispered something in Dylan's ear. Seth, in turn, said something to them both.

"Where did you two disappear to this afternoon?"

Kerri smiled shyly at Dylan and let him answer.

"We were at the beach mostly."

"Who with?"

"Each other," Dylan said. "We had some things to talk about."

"Like, how you're going to handle a long-distance relationship?"

Kerri smiled and blushed. "Uh-oh," she said, leaning into Dylan's shoulder and giving him a wonderfully sweet expression. "I think we got caught."

"It was your idea to let me kiss you right there in plain sight," Dylan said, speaking to Kerri in a way Amber had never seen anyone speak to her—not even Dylan in the past.

Looking back to her brother, Kerri spoke in her normal tone. "We've got nothing to hide. Isn't that what you always say, Seth?"

"Yes, and I think it's great," he said. "That's why we didn't interrupt."

"Didn't interrupt what?" Matt said, breaking in on their conversation.

"Would you like to tell him, or should I?" Seth asked his sister.

Kerri turned to Matt, who was sitting on her left, and she answered for herself. "Dylan and I have decided to keep seeing each other, and my sweet brother caught us kissing this afternoon."

"When?" Matt asked. "We were with you two the whole time."

"They were on the beach. I think your eyes were elsewhere."

Matt smiled, and Kerri leaned over to whisper something in his ear. He got an intrigued look on his face. "Yeah?" he said.

"Oh, yeah," Kerri assured him.

Amber watched curiously as Matt seemed to contemplate something. He finally got out of his chair, came around the table to where Mandy was sitting beside her and whispered something that Amber heard.

"Can I talk to you outside for a minute?"

"Sure," Mandy said, appearing delighted and curious about his request.

After they were gone, Amber asked Kerri, "What did you say to him?"

She smiled and glanced up at Dylan. "I said, 'A girl can never say no to a kiss on the beach.'"

Chapter Twelve

By the time their pizza was ready fifteen minutes later, Matt and Mandy had not returned. They were only a block away from the beach, and Amber was about to go out of her mind wondering if that's where Matt had taken her and what was happening.

"Should I go look for them?" Seth asked. "Let them know the pizza is ready?"

"I'll go with you," she said.

They left the restaurant and looked around the immediate area but didn't see them anywhere. Walking toward the beach, Amber asked Seth if Matt had said anything to him today about Mandy, and Seth said he'd only made a few brief comments about Mandy starting to open up more and how much he was enjoying his time with her.

Scanning the wide sandy beach when they reached the end of the street, Amber didn't see them anywhere nearby and neither did Seth. "Are you worried?" Seth asked her.

"No, I'm not worried," she said. "I'm just wondering where they are."

"Let's go back," he said, taking her hand and not giving her much choice in the matter. "We'll save them some pizza if they don't make it back in time."

Amber supposed that was all they could do. She wasn't worried about Mandy being alone with Matt, but when another twenty minutes went by, and they still saw no sign of them,

Amber started to become a little concerned, but only because they were going to be leaving soon.

When the group leaders stood up to announce it was time to head for the vans and they were leaving in fifteen minutes, she and Seth decided to go look for them once again, but they didn't have to go far once they stepped outside. Matt and Mandy were coming down the sidewalk toward them from the beach, and they were holding hands.

"Did we miss dinner?" Matt asked, flashing a crooked smile.

"Yeah, man. You sort of did," Seth said, holding a take-home box in his hand. "We saved some for you though."

Amber caught Mandy's eye, and her cousin appeared happy. They all began walking toward where the vans were parked, and Mandy didn't separate from Matt until they reached the restrooms adjacent to the parking area. She followed her and Kerri into the women's side, and Amber wasted no time in asking her a question.

"What did he say?" she whispered.

"I'll tell you later," she whispered back.

Amber respected her privacy and didn't demand an explanation with Kerri and other girls from the youth group all around. But she held Mandy back once they were outside again and it was just the two of them.

"Are you okay?"

"Yes," Mandy smiled, letting out a happy sigh.

"Did he kiss you?"

She nodded.

Amber saw Seth and Matt waiting for them on the sidewalk, and she stopped asking questions. They crossed the street to find seats in one of the vans, and Matt told Mandy he would help her find an open front seat, but Mandy reached for his hand and said, "I'd rather sit with you."

"Are you sure you'll be all right?"

"Yes," she said. "As long as we're not way in the back."

"If you start to feel sick, let me know, all right?"

"I will," she said. "I won't throw up on you, I promise."

"I'm not worried about me."

Mandy didn't respond to his caring words, but she wasn't oblivious to them either. She got into the van and sat by the window in the front bench seat, and Matt sat beside her. Amber and Seth took the seat behind them, but Mandy and Matt were in their own little world for the next two hours.

Amber and Mandy had planned to catch a MAX train home when they returned to Portland, but Matt and Seth suggested they stay through tomorrow afternoon. After calling their parents to ask if that was okay, Amber and Mandy spent the remainder of the evening with Seth, Matt, Kerri, and Dylan. Dylan left at eleven, and Kerri walked him out and didn't return for a little while. Matt left at midnight, and Mandy stepped outside to say good-night to him, and she didn't return immediately either.

Once she and Mandy were in Kerri's room for the night, Mandy gave her a hug and held on for a long time. "You were right, Amber."

"Right about what?"

"That the right guy would like me just for who I am."

Amber stepped back and smiled. "Did he tell you that?"

"Yes. And I have no idea how he knew I needed to hear that, but when we went down to the beach together, he started talking and said all the right things."

"What's the best thing he said?"

"Besides, 'I'd really like to kiss you'?"

Amber laughed. "Besides that."

She thought for a moment. "He said after he broke up with Clarissa and got his life straight with God again, he sat down and made a list of the qualities he was looking for in a girlfriend, and I'm the first girl to meet every single one of them. He also said I have others he wasn't looking for but knows he needs."

"Do you feel that way about him? Is he the ideal guy for you?"

"Yes, I think he is."

"And I'm guessing the kissing isn't too bad either?"

Mandy smiled. "He's the first guy I've ever kissed, Amber."

"I thought so."

"It was amazing. I never expected to feel like that."

Amber had the feeling Mandy would rather keep the more intimate details of her time with Matt to herself, and she didn't ask any more questions. But Mandy did tell her one more thing after she had turned out the light and gotten into bed beside her.

"He wants me to meet his parents tomorrow. Did you know his dad is one of the pastors at the church?"

"Yes. Did you?"

"Not until he told me tonight."

Mandy sounded apprehensive about meeting their approval. "I'm sure his parents will be thrilled to have him dating someone like you."

"But I didn't bring a dress or anything remotely nice."

Amber smiled, recalling her own insecurities about meeting Seth's parents for the first time. That seemed like a long time ago. Now she had far greater concerns—like how they would react if Seth announced they were getting married so soon after graduation.

"Don't worry about it, Mandy," she said. "You've waited for the right guy. Now that you've found him, just enjoy it. Let him get to know the real you. Don't hold anything back. Be who you are, and believe that's who Matt wants. And above all, surrender yourself and this relationship to Jesus. If you do that, He will make it exactly as it should be."

As Amber spoke, she was reminded she needed to do the same in her relationship with Seth in adding this surprising new twist that had come about in forty-eight hours.

The following day Mandy did seem to enjoy her time with Matt, and meeting his parents went fine. Matt was nothing but sweet with her, and it amazed Amber to see him so in tune with her slow and quiet pace.

If he was talking with someone else, he was loud and laughing and being Mr. Personality, which is the way he had always been as long as Amber had known him. But when he was with Mandy, he talked less and in a more tender way, and yet it was completely him, not like he was trying to be someone he wasn't. Mandy brought out a side of him no one else could, and he seemed to do the same for her.

He kissed her good-bye at the MAX station, and he didn't hold anything back because they weren't alone on the beach. It was the first time Amber had seen them kiss, and it made her smile. She turned her eyes away and caught Seth watching them also. He smiled too and gave her his own sweet kisses that had taken on a new quality this weekend.

On the way home Mandy was a little worried about everything being different the next time she saw Matt. She loved the way he made her feel, and she didn't want it to go away or discover their time together didn't mean as much to him as it did to her.

"He's not like that, Mandy. He wanted to be so careful about this. He wanted to make sure it was right before he did anything to let you know how much he liked you."

"How do you know that?"

"I'm dating his best friend, sweetie. I had the inside scoop."

"And you didn't tell me?"

"If anyone was going to be telling you anything, I knew it should be Matt."

"I'm so scared, Amber. Am I ready for this?"

"I think you are. Don't be afraid of it. God brought you together. He had you going to the same college before you even met. If He's in this, and I think you know He is, you'll be all right—even if it doesn't work out with Matt, God will be preparing you for someone else."

"But I don't want anyone else."

"I know," she laughed. "I felt the same way. One day at a time—that's all you can do, and today was a pretty good day, wasn't it?"

She smiled. "Yes."

"Then focus on that. Think about his kisses all week. Guys who aren't trying to get anything more can't fake kisses like that."

Amber hesitated to share what entered her mind, but she went ahead, knowing it could help Mandy with her insecurities. "I saw Matt kiss Clarissa when they were together, and he doesn't kiss you the same way. It's completely different, trust me."

"Were they having sex? Do you know?"

"I don't think so, but you'll have to ask Matt if you really want to know."

"Do you think I should ask him that?"

"Yes. I think you should."

Mandy gave her a look that made her laugh.

"Welcome to the world of dating, my sweet cousin."

"Okay, never mind. Tell Matt I decided to become a nun."

"No way! He is going to fall so completely in love with you. I know it, Mandy. Wait and see."

Mandy didn't reply, and Amber knew why.

"You're already falling in love, aren't you?"

110

"Yes," she whispered. "That's stupid, right?"

"No, Mandy. It's not stupid. It's brave, but don't keep your feelings from Matt. Don't hide them. Every time I take a risk and tell Seth something that seems scary, or he does that with me, it brings us closer."

"Will you pray for me?"

She smiled and gave her a hug. "I already have been, and I won't stop. I promise."

Amber had an email from Loralyn waiting for her when she arrived home, and it was a really long one. Lora said she'd had a difficult week and had almost called off her engagement with Eric because she wasn't sure she was ready to get married. Their career plans didn't seem to be meshing very well, and this time she had lost sight of what was most important—their love for each other. But God had intervened and made her see that once again. She ended the message by saying:

My grandpa told me he's learned the key to life is believing in God's love, loving Him in return, and loving others, like Jesus tells us. I've heard that all my life, but I'm finally realizing how true that really is. And I've decided that's all I need to be concerned about. The rest will work itself out, but only I can choose to love and be loved. One thing I did to help me see just how much God loves me is I made a list of all the ways God has blessed me and met my needs through those around me. It was a really long list! I encourage you to do the same.

Amber responded to her message and then did what Lora suggested, taking her journal out and making a list of all the ways God had shown His love to her. And when she finished, one of the things she was reminded of was God would be faithful to guide her and Seth in this new decision they had to make. His guidance would be based on His love for both of them, and they could trust however He led them on this new path.

She had given others advice about getting married: Stacey, Lora, and Hope. But now that it was her, she realized what a huge decision it was—even more so than what college to go to. It would be the biggest and most important decision of her life, and she knew exactly what she needed to do: Pray.

God, I love Seth. I want to marry him someday. But when is the right time? Please give us wisdom. Guide us clearly and help us to listen and to do what you say is best. Right now my head is telling me it's too soon, that we should wait two or three years, but all weekend my heart was telling me something different. Show us the path YOU have for us, and help us to trust you. I surrender myself and our relationship to you. Help me to remain there. Help me to be still and wait to hear YOUR voice.

Chapter Thirteen

Amber's thoughts turned to her cousin, and she wrote out a prayer for Mandy and Matt. She had been praying for them for several weeks now, and she felt at peace about what had happened between them this weekend and the future of their relationship. She wasn't sure why. She just did, and she chose to believe she didn't need to worry about Mandy getting her heart broken or them going too far physically, or any of the dozens of things that could go wrong. She wondered if that was because she had already been praying and God was giving her peace. She remembered feeling the same about Lora after she had gotten back together with Eric, and even though the road hadn't been easy for them, it was obvious God was guiding them each step of the way.

On Monday afternoon Amber went to softball practice, and her coach wanted to talk to her. He told her there had been a college scout at the game on Friday. He'd actually been there to watch some of the players on the opposing team, but he had been very impressed with her pitching and was interested in meeting her and offering her a scholarship to play for Washington State University.

"Tell him thanks," she said, not thinking twice about it, "but I've already decided what school I'm going to."

"You could just talk to him," he said.

Amber knew her coach wasn't a Christian. He was a great coach and a good teacher. She'd had him for *Earth Science* her freshman year and *Biology* her sophomore year, and she wasn't great at science in general, but he had done a good job of explaining complicated things and making labs interesting and fun.

But she'd heard him say many times that evolution was the only explanation that fit the geologic record, and he outright dismissed Creation, saying, 'I know many of you have been taught God made the world in six days, but forget that. It's a fairy tale, not reality.'

Back then she hadn't known enough to argue with him. She'd learned some things since to help her see how scientific facts did support Creation. It was all a matter of how the "evidence" was interpreted. She had been praying for him and other science teachers who had similar beliefs, that God could somehow reach them with the truth. She hadn't had the opportunity to discuss scientific issues with him, but she did know God was at work in her life, and she responded with what she knew to be true.

"I'm sure playing for Washington State is a great opportunity, but God already showed me which school I'm supposed to go to."

"Are you going to be playing softball for them?"

"They don't have a team."

"And why exactly are you going there? Because that's where your boyfriend wants to go?"

"No. Because that's where God wants both of us to go."

"God wants you to go there? And you know this because?"

She smiled. "Because He told me so."

"You could be throwing away a great college softball career, Wilson."

"And that's important because—?"

He didn't have a response for that.

114

"There's a lot more to my life than sports," she said. "Not the least of which is getting to know my God and going where He leads me."

He didn't have a response for that either.

"Was there anything else, or can I go warm up now?"

"Nope, nothing else," he said. "We've got four games left this season; let's make the most of them."

"I'd love to," she said, putting on her glove and catching the ball he tossed at her. She added one more thing. "You've been a great coach. I've had a lot of fun."

"I've noticed," he said, following her onto the field. "What happened to that incredibly talented but timid girl who used to crack under pressure her sophomore year?"

She laughed. "Jesus took her to the high places," she said, jogging away from him to go throw some pitches to Stacey.

They played well on Wednesday, beating a mid-ranked team in their league, and then on Friday they had to play Centennial again, but on their field this time. If they could somehow pull off a win against the undefeated team and win their next two games also, they would make it into the playoffs for the first time in her years on varsity. She wasn't overly optimistic, but she planned to give it her best shot.

Seth and Matt drove out for the game, and Mandy came too. Seth and Matt were going to be spending the night at her house, and Ben and Hope were coming tonight also. Matt had called Mandy every night this week, and tomorrow Matt was going to be meeting Mandy's mom and dad.

Amber pitched well—almost as good as last Friday, but some of her teammates weren't on with their hitting, so they ended up losing the game, but she had fun anyway. Almost every time they had lost this season, or she hadn't played her best, God always brought Seth's words to mind he had spoken after the first volleyball game she'd had to sit in the stands to watch: *You matter to Me.* She had stopped judging herself for her achievements and efforts, choosing instead to believe she was loved and valued by God and others, no matter what.

Stacey was a little down on herself because she hadn't had a hit all night, and she had also allowed a run to score when she dropped the ball at home plate. She had seen Kenny last weekend in Corvallis when she went to see his Saturday game and spent the rest of the day with him, but he was traveling to eastern Washington tonight for a game tomorrow, and she had been missing him terribly all week as it was. Amber recognized the signs, and before she went to leave and find Seth, she whispered in her ear. "Only one more month to go and Kenny is all yours."

She looked at her and a smile came to her face. "Can't you see I'm in a bad mood here? Why did you have to go and say that?"

"Because it's just a game, Stace. And Kenny would be the first to tell you so if he was here."

Stacey hugged her and held on. "I'm glad we're going to camp with you. I'm not ready to say good-bye yet."

"Me neither."

"All right," she said, laughing and stepping away like this conversation was getting too mushy for her. "Go hug that boyfriend of yours now."

She laughed. "Okay. Have a nice weekend. See you on Sunday."

She turned away to go meet Seth and smacked right into him. He had snuck up behind her, and his sudden presence made for quite the greeting.

"Where are you off to in such a hurry?" he said, laughing as he caught his balance and kept them both from falling over.

She smiled. "I was coming to meet you."

"Me? Do I know you?"

"I'm your girlfriend," she said, giving him a sweet kiss.

"All right," Stacey interrupted. "There's way too much love around here. Let the lonely girl by."

Seth reached out and stopped Stacey from stepping past them. "Hang on, Blondie," he said. "Some guy's here who wants to know if you will go out with him tonight."

"Is that supposed to be funny?" she asked, not hiding her sarcasm.

"No," Seth said. "But it's supposed to make you smile."

Stacey wasn't amused, and Amber wondered why Seth had said that. It wasn't like him to tease Stacey this way. He knew she wasn't the type who took teasing well. But before Seth or Stacey said anything else, Amber heard a voice behind her that caught Stacey's attention immediately.

"Hey, beautiful."

They both looked and saw Kenny standing there. Amber smiled. Tears came to her friend's eyes, and Stacey stepped toward him, but she didn't completely break out of her current mood.

"What are you doing here?"

Her words didn't keep Kenny from greeting her with his classic smile and lifting Stacey off the ground as he hugged her. After giving her a few kisses, he spoke to them over her shoulder. "I think I just got myself a date. You two up for pizza tonight?"

"Sounds good to me," Seth said, steering her away from them for the moment. "We'll meet you out there."

They left to give them some privacy, and Amber asked why Kenny was here instead of in Washington. Seth said he'd hurt his knee during practice yesterday. Not too seriously but enough that his coach wanted him to stay here and rest it this weekend instead of traveling with the team. She also asked where Matt and Mandy were when she didn't see them waiting nearby.

"They're probably in the parking lot. Matt drove tonight."

"Was he anxious to see her?"

"Yes. She's all he could talk about all week. He's falling for her fast, and he's scared to death, but he's not backing off unless she doesn't feel the same way."

"She feels the same way."

"So I guessed. I've never heard her talk as much as she did tonight."

When they reached the parking lot, Amber spotted them beside Matt's car, and they were still talking. She stopped Seth to give them more time alone and also to ask him something.

"Mandy asked me if Matt and Clarissa were having sex, and I said I didn't know. Do you?"

"They didn't," he said with certainty. "Matt's never been with anybody."

"It sounds like you've talked about this."

"Yes. One of the things Matt said to me after he broke up with Clarissa was he knew God had rescued him at just the right time, and he asked me why God would do that for him, and I said, 'He did it for you and Clarissa because He loves you both, and He also did it for the girl you're really meant to be with.'"

Chapter Fourteen

After having pizza with Stacey and Kenny, they took Mandy home and then Matt drove out to her house. Ben and Hope were there when they arrived. It only took Amber a second to know Ben and Hope were officially engaged. Besides the ring on Hope's finger, their smiles and peaceful expressions gave them away.

She went to Hope first and hugged her for a long time. It had been this same time last year Hope had told her about Ben kissing her for the first time, and she had a peaceful feeling that God had truly healed Hope from her past hurts and set her free to love and be loved by Ben in every way.

She hugged Ben also, and tears came to her eyes. Recalling the conversation she'd had with Ben the night he had first heard all Hope had been through, she knew his plan to "just love her" had been the right path to take. Ben had chosen to love deeply regardless of the risk involved, and in return he had become deeply loved by a young woman who had so much to give him.

In the morning when Amber came downstairs, Seth, Ben, and Matt had gone somewhere, she learned from her dad who was at the kitchen table reading a fishing magazine. Amber hadn't known when Seth planned to talk to both of them about keeping him accountable this summer to the no-kissing policy they had agreed upon, and also in keeping their alone-time to a minimum, but she knew that's likely what he was doing.

He confirmed that later after they returned and Matt was on the phone with Mandy. Matt had called to let her know they were on their way to her house but ended up talking to her for several minutes, giving her and Seth a private moment.

"I told them what we talked about, and they both said they would be watching me closely and asking me regularly about our time together, and Ben is going to talk to Hope about possibly doing the same, although he's doing a lot better now, and he's not sure he can commit to not kissing his fiancée.

"I think it's a little different for them. They're more used to being together every day and have been on their own for almost a year now."

"Yes, and they need to decide what's right for them," he said and whispered in her ear. "Just like we have to decide if getting married this year is the right thing for us."

She smiled at him but didn't say anything. She had been thinking about it off and on but wasn't feeling anything definite at this point. A week ago she had a lot of anxiety about making the decision, but now she felt at peace. She believed God would show them what was right.

On the drive in to meet Mandy, Matt was unusually quiet, and Amber knew he was nervous about meeting her family. But he presented himself well once they arrived, and Uncle Tom and Aunt Beth welcomed him easily.

The four of them had a fun day together, and Amber knew her senior year was coming to a bittersweet end. She was looking forward to finishing school, but she was going to miss many of her friends and playing softball. It had been very fun this year. She still had the summer with Stacey and Colleen, but she would be saying good-bye to them along with Ben and Hope, her parents, and her camp friends at the end of the summer.

On the other hand, she and Seth were still together, and she didn't imagine that would be changing. Matt and Mandy were beginning what appeared to be a promising relationship. And she was looking forward to going away to college with them, along with Kerri, Jessica, and possibly Chad. He hadn't made his final decision yet, but Seth seemed to think it was going to happen.

The four of them ended the day by going to the lake. They stayed together at first, but they were all a little surprised when Mandy interrupted a silent moment by saying, "Can I talk to you for a minute, Matt?"

"Sure," he said, coming to a stop along with Mandy. "You two go ahead. We'll catch up."

"What do you think that's about?" Seth asked after they had distanced themselves from them.

"I'm not sure," she said, thinking of several possibilities but not sharing any of them directly. She was trying hard not to say too much to Seth that Mandy had told her privately.

Mandy and Matt didn't catch back up with them until after they had returned to the parking lot. It was getting late by then, and Matt drove them back to her house where Seth said good night to her there. He and Matt were planning to take Mandy home too and then drive back to Portland tonight.

At nine-thirty her mom came upstairs where she was attempting to get some homework done and said there was a phone call for her.

"Who is it?" she asked, reaching for the extension in her room and seeing the concerned look on her mom's face.

"Colleen. She sounds upset."

Amber clicked on the phone and said hello. Her mom was right. Colleen could barely speak.

"What's wrong?"

She let out a pained sigh. "Chris and I broke up."

"What? Why?"

Amber hoped this was a small problem they were having that would resolve itself, but the more Colleen talked, the more she knew that wasn't the case. Chris had decided he wanted to go to Vietnam for a year. He would be going to China this summer on the mission trip, and then he could go live with his grandparents in Hanoi and go to school there to learn Vietnamese and teach English. It was a huge opportunity for him, and he felt God calling him to go now while he could, knowing this could open more doors for him there in the future.

Colleen supported his decision and agreed he needed to do this, but neither of them expected each other to continue as they were for a whole year with Chris gone. They had come to this decision together, and it didn't necessarily mean they would never see each other again, but Colleen was very upset and feeling lost about her own future. She had decided to go to Bible college next year at Multnomah with Chris, but now he wasn't going to be there.

"I feel so empty and lost, Amber. My entire world just stopped."

"I can't imagine, Colleen," she said. "I'm sorry."

They were both silent for a moment and then Amber said, "There's a reason, Colleen. For all of it."

"I know, and the strange thing is I don't regret any of our time together. I know I'll miss him, but I don't think it's the way you would feel if you lost Seth. I enjoyed our relationship for what it was, but I could never picture forever, and now I know why."

"Do you still feel going to Multnomah is the right place for you?"

"I'm not sure. I'll have to pray about it, I guess."

Amber's immediate thought was that Colleen could go to Lifegate instead, but she didn't say anything. She would let

Colleen talk to God about it first and give her input later if Colleen seemed indecisive.

Amber hesitated to tell Mandy about Colleen's news the following afternoon when they went to her grandmother's for Sunday lunch, simply because this wasn't the best time for Mandy to be hearing about a relationship ending, but it wasn't like she could hide the news forever. Mandy would be seeing Colleen herself on Monday.

She told her and then waited for Mandy's reaction. "Didn't they break up once before?"

"Yes. About this same time last year, actually, but then they got back together over the summer when Chris decided to go to school here."

"Do you think it's really over this time?"

"Hard to say. If Chris comes back next year and Colleen isn't with anyone else, I can see them getting back together. But we'll have to wait and see."

"What would you do?"

"If Seth announced he was going to be gone for a year?"

"Yes."

"I don't know. I know I'd miss him, but I can't imagine being with anyone else. If he was leaving for good, that would be different, but if I knew he was coming back, I think I'd just wait for him."

Mandy smiled, and she asked what that was for.

"I'm sad for Colleen, really. But what you just said reminded me of something Matt said to me last night."

"At the lake?"

She nodded.

"What did you want to talk to him about, or is that just between the two of you?"

"I got really brave, Amber, and I asked him about some of the things we talked about on the way home last weekend."

"You mean about Clarissa?"

"Yes, I asked him about her—what their relationship was like; if he loved her; why it didn't work out—and when I got the answers I wanted to hear about all that, I told him I have no clue what I'm doing with a guy like him. He said he feels so different about me and that he's never kissed a girl like he kisses me, and then I said, 'And I've never kissed a guy, period, Matthew Abramson.' And you should have seen the look on his face!"

Amber laughed. "What did he say?"

"First he said he felt unworthy of being the source of my first kiss, but then he said it confirms for him that God has brought me into his life, and he said, 'Are you going to wait for me over the summer or fall for some other guy at camp?'"

"And what did you say?"

"I said, 'I'll be waiting for you every Saturday.'"

"Does this news about Chris and Colleen scare you?"

"I'm already scared," she laughed. "It doesn't make much difference."

"What do you like best about him, now that you've gotten to know him better?"

She thought for a moment and then replied. "He likes me for who I am, and I like everything about him, but I know there's so much below the surface I haven't discovered yet."

"He lets you see sides of him no one else sees," she said. "I've already noticed that."

Mandy smiled again. "You know something he told me yesterday?"

"What?"

"We had been talking nonstop for about thirty minutes while we were walking around the lake, and then we were both quiet the rest of the way, and he said how much he loved that."

"That you're quiet?"

"Yes, and that he can be quiet with me."

Amber could relate because she felt the same way about enjoying Mandy's company without always having to be talking, and she knew she felt that way with Seth too. "Some of my favorite times with Seth are when we're both being quiet. Feeling content with each other without having to add anything to it."

"That's one of the things that amazes me. I really enjoy being with him no matter what we're doing—especially when it's just the two of us, and I've never felt comfortable with a guy like that before. And I feel like of all guys, Matt should make me the most nervous, but he doesn't—even when I first met him at the retreat, I felt relaxed whenever he talked to me."

"I know what you mean," Amber said. "Even when I had just dumped Pepsi on Seth and I didn't even know him, he still managed to make me smile."

Chapter Fifteen

The following Saturday was Mandy's eighteenth birthday, and Mandy chose to spend the day with her friends at the beach. It had been Matt's idea for a bunch of them to go—basically whomever Mandy wanted to invite, but she kept the guest-list small. Two of her longtime friends from Eugene were going to meet them in Newport, and she also invited her and Seth, along with Colleen, Nicole, and Stacey, but Stacey was going to Kenny's final games of the season in Corvallis this weekend. Nicole asked Spencer to meet them there, and it was a really fun day from Amber's perspective.

Mandy was more the center of attention than usual, mainly because everyone else knew she wouldn't put herself there and kept insisting this was her day and they were going to do whatever she wanted to do. But Amber could see being with Matt gave her cousin more confidence in herself and made her more outgoing than normal. Amber loved watching them together. Matt was sweet and perfect. He never did anything to embarrass Mandy, but he knew how to tease her in the right way to make it fun, and he always seemed to know when she needed something specific from him—like a brief kiss, a quiet moment, or a playful one.

They all went to the aquarium, and shopping along the Bay, and down to the beach, and out for a nice dinner—but no matter where they were, Matt was by Mandy's side. It was obvious he saw his mission for the day as making her feel as special as possible, and he was definitely succeeding.

"Have you been coaching him all week on how to make a girl feel like the most special person in the world?" Amber asked Seth when they went for a final walk on the beach after dinner. Matt and Mandy were about twenty paces in front of them, and when they stopped to share a tender kiss, she and Seth stopped also.

"No, not really," Seth said. "With the right girl I think it comes naturally."

"Is he going to give her his present now or wait until tomorrow?"

"I think now," Seth said, glancing their direction. Matt and Mandy started walking away from them a bit more, but they remained in place. "We'll give him space to do that."

Amber was more than happy to remain in place and enjoy some sweet kisses, even if she would like to see Mandy's reaction to Matt's gift. He was following his best friend's lead and giving Mandy something for her birthday to symbolize his commitment to keep their relationship pure. Only instead of giving Mandy a bracelet, he was giving her a ring with a small heart in the center of the band. Amber had gotten a sneak-peek last night when Matt and Seth had come out to the house to spend the night after her softball game.

Her softball season was officially over. If they would have won one more game they could have made it into the playoffs, but in a way Amber was glad they hadn't. She was feeling really burned out on school and her busy schedule. She was ready to graduate in two weeks, have one relaxing week at home, and then head off to camp for the summer.

"Colleen seems to be in good spirits today," Seth said. "Do you think she's okay or just faking it?"

"I think she's okay. Chris called her a couple of times this week, and they had some good talks. Colleen feels like it might not be completely over, but if it turns out to be, she has peace that God has other plans for both of them. I think right now her main concern is if she's making the right decision about school. She still feels like she should go to Multnomah for at least a year, but her dad is encouraging her to go to U of O."

"Did you talk to her about going to Lifegate?"

"Yes. And she's thought about it too, but she feels like God wouldn't have brought her and Chris together for no reason, and getting her to Multnomah may be it. And I agree with her. I know for a fact she never would have considered going there otherwise. She had her plans all in place since sophomore year, but I can see God stepping in and redirecting her path."

Seth was silent for a moment and then said thoughtfully, "It's funny how God works. He uses Chris and Colleen's relationship to get them where they need to be—which isn't necessarily together, and then He confirms for Kerri she's on the right path by giving her a boyfriend who won't be in California with her, but somehow she knows both Dylan and Lifegate are a part of her future plans, coexisting even though it doesn't seem like they should go together."

"And then there's us," she said. "Separated for two years and together at the same time. I can't believe we only have two more weeks to go."

"Are you having any doubts about going to California and continuing our relationship, Amber? Any at all?"

"No. Are you?"

"No," he said softly. "I've had this steady peace ever since Christmas—except for my 48 hours of emotional distress you put me through."

She smiled. "Well, it couldn't be too perfect. Every relationship has to have one or two bumps in it."

"I'd prefer no more bumps, okay?"

She laughed. "Okay."

"I'm not going anywhere, Amber, and I'm holding on tight now. I don't want anyone else. I want you to know that. I want you to believe it with all of your heart, even if we decide not to get married for awhile."

She knew Seth meant what he said, and she felt the same way about him.

"Do you know that?" he asked.

"Yes."

"Even with Chris and Colleen breaking up?"

"Yes. I almost lost you two months ago, and I know I never want to consider that ever again. I tried to say good-bye to you, but I couldn't. And now I feel more in love with you than ever. And if you were the only piece of my life that wasn't going to be changing—if I had to let go of everything else but I still had you—that would be enough for me."

He smiled. "Have you been talking to God about me behind my back?"

She laughed. "What?"

"I was a mess this week, Amber. After I heard about Chris and Colleen, I kept trying to tell myself we were okay, but I couldn't believe it until God told me something about an hour ago."

"What did He tell you?"

"We were sitting at the table in the restaurant, and you were talking to Mandy, and I was watching you, thinking about our day together and wishing it didn't have to end, and then I heard God whisper to my heart: 'Your life is changing, Seth. It's going to change a lot after graduation. You'll be going to new places and meeting new people and doing new things. But Amber is yours—indefinitely. I promise.'"

A warm feeling swept through Amber's entire being, and she smiled. "Jesus told you that?"

"Yes, I believe He did. Is that okay with you?"

"Yes."

He took her into his arms and held her close. She could feel his heart beating slowly and steadily, like he was completely at peace with the enormity of what he had just said to her.

"If I'm yours indefinitely," she said softly, "that means you're mine indefinitely too, right?"

He laughed. "I believe that's how it works."

"Have you been praying about what we're supposed to be praying about?"

"Yes."

"And?"

"I'm still praying."

She didn't reply.

"In a million years, Amber, I never thought I'd be considering it at all before graduation."

"Did you ever imagine we would be where we are now when you took me on that canoe ride?"

"No. I knew I liked you, but I never imagined you would invade my heart like you have."

He kissed her gently and didn't stop until Matt and Mandy returned. Amber felt dizzy. She and Seth had been in a different world. She had no idea how much time had passed but didn't feel embarrassed they had been caught.

"All right, man," Matt said. "Enough of that. You were the one who said we should get out of here by eight."

They had ridden with Matt and Mandy, and they returned to Portland in the same way. Nicole had driven also, and Colleen rode with her. Amber fell asleep on Seth's shoulder somewhere between Corvallis and Seth's house. Nicole and

Colleen were driving back to Sandy tonight, but she and Mandy spent the night at Seth's.

In the morning they went to church, and Amber felt God speaking to her during the message, bringing a mixture of peace, uncertainty, and excitement. The title of the message was: "Listening to the Spirit", and it was all about recognizing God's voice and believing we have the ability to do so.

The pastor read from 1 Corinthians 2:9-10. *"'No eye has seen, no ear has heard, and no mind has imagined what God has prepared for those who love him.' But we know these things because God has revealed them to us by his Spirit, and his Spirit searches out everything and shows us even God's deep secrets."*

Amber knew the words could refer to many aspects of her life; from understanding and knowing God better, to what God had planned for her regarding school, her future career, and ministry opportunities. But right now she was most consumed with what the coming months would hold for her and Seth as a couple. Would they be getting married later this year? Was that foolish or exactly what God had planned? And most of all, how were they supposed to know?

But the verses from the Bible told her they could know, because God knew, and He could show them through His Spirit that lived within both of their hearts. Her feelings of assurance on that were confirmed when Seth wrote something on his notes and passed the paper to her, sharing his thoughts:

He will show us, baby. We <u>can</u> know what God has planned.

*I'd love to hear how God has used
this story to touch your heart.*

Write me at:

living_loved@yahoo.com

Made in the USA
Middletown, DE
15 May 2015